SILENCERS

PROLOGUE

▼

Leon Maseklos could still feel a painful stiffness in his knees as he walked. That was understandable. Considering the fact that he had just awoke from a frozen sleep of nearly three hundred years. His body still shivered against the cold air of this massive ship's dark corridor. He regret that he did not choose an additional garment to bolster the grey coveralls that he wore. But he expected to soon disregard the cold as his excitement mounted.

There was only one reason why he was awakened from his long slumber. Robotic probes launched from the ship have finally discovered a suitable planet for colonization. As the head of this expedition it was his duty and privilege to be awakened first. After he confirmed the probe's findings he would awaken several key crew members from their cryo-suspension tubes. Then the work of colonization could begin. Aboard this ship were thousands of passengers. All frozen in a centuries long sleep while waiting for a chance to meet their new world.

There were six other vessels identical to this huge rectangular ship. Each one carrying a large cargo of sleeping passengers. They were part of an expedition fleet who's mission was to relocate the select Human populace of Earth to a new home. Leon could vividly recall the tales of the historic and terrible events that set the stage for this Human migration. In 2059 a gargantuan mass of jagged metal and ice entered Earth's star system without any advance warning. Measuring over forty miles in diameter the intruder purposefully sped past Jupiter and Mars on a direct course to it's intended target. The Earth itself.

Reports have stated that the object impacted with the ground with a force that surpassed a nuclear explosion. A major city and a huge portion of it's metropolitan area were obliterated. The horrendous death toll was too high for anyone to accurately count. Earth's environment was soon plunged into a global winter effect as tons of soot and debris from the blast formed thick clouds that blocked out the life giving sunlight.

The worst disaster came a month later when a mysterious viral outbreak quickly spread throughout the Human populace. It's victims suffered fatigue and loss of muscle coordination. Paranoia and psychotic behavior soon followed. It's most horrible effect was infesting it's victims faces with bleeding cold blisters. A majority of it's victims died within ten days. It was largely believed that the viral organism was somehow released into the atmosphere by the object. But that theory was never scientifically proven. Because of it's ghastly symptoms the illness was named the Pandora Simplex.

Earth's scientists committed a global effort to find an effective serum against the virus, but they were hopelessly stymied. Within a year forty five percent of the Human population was dead. Unsuspecting travelers even carried the virus to the numerous colonies that were established on the planet Mars. The virus and the frigid conditions on Earth were threatening to exterminate the Human species. Their only hope for survival was to turn to the deep space exploration program that was being developed. Thousands of healthy volunteers were gathered and placed under strict quarantine aboard space stations orbiting Earth and Mars. A fleet of huge oblong ships were constructed and loaded with the necessary supplies and equipment to build new worlds. Then in 2069 the surviving Humans began their mission to find a new home. Six separate fleets of ships disembarking for different destinations in the vast darkness of space. An event that led to Leon Maseklos on this pivotal day.

The door to the ship's main bridge slid open for Leon. He strode past several rows of instrument consoles to reach the data analysis station. With the touch of several buttons he summoned the desired information onto a monitor. The long ranged probes had indeed discovered a suitable planet. It's mass appeared to be slightly larger than that of earth. Several mountainous land formations were separated by a global body of water. The atmospheric composition was within the desired parameters. Large amounts of oxygen mixed with nitrogen and a small amount of argon. Present temperature, seventy two degrees. Soil and water analysis yielded no toxic materials or potentially harmful microorganisms. Least of all anything as deadly as the Pandora Simplex.

Leon nodded in satisfaction. This would be the world where Human civilization would get a fresh start. Now after all these years in a deep cold sleep the members of this expedition team would awaken to the challenge of establishing a colony, then building the first of many cities across this planet. During the construction the exploration of deep space would continue. If there were other hospitable planets out there then they would be claimed as well. And perhaps this team could establish contact with the other five teams that embarked on their own journey. Leon wondered if it was possible that his team could be the first to discover a new home. The other teams could still be traveling somewhere out in deep space. Their Human cargo remaining asleep until they finally received the signal that Leon awakened to. Or it was possible that one or more teams could have already established themselves on newly discovered planets. That was a mystery that Leon hoped would be solved within his lifetime. But for now he would concentrate on being one of the first Humans to step foot upon the soil of their new homeworld.

C H A P T E R 1

▼

"Does it always rain on this damn planet?" Sergeant Colin McKenzie asked himself.

The young black male sprinted across the soggy forest, accompanied by the other members of his platoon. His hands maintained a firm grip on his AR-20 laser rifle. He silently cursed the heavy plastic body armor that he wore. Colored dark camouflage green to match his rain soaked fatigues. It's thickness might provide his torso with a limited degree of protection but it's weight restricted his movements.

This heavy downpour was also working against Colin. It was irritating, the way that the raindrops continuously pelted his helmet and face. That made it difficult for him to see his destination. Of all the planets in the United Protectorate Colin was unlucky enough to be exiled to Meridan during this war. A sparsely populated planet who's environment was comprised of weed ridden fields and swamps infested by hoards of insects and parasites. The climate was always chilly. The average temperature was in the low fifties. Although Colin felt that the frequent rains made the climate feel much colder.

Colin's platoon was getting closer to their destination. He joined the other troopers as they took cover behind trees and shrubbery. Colin dove to the ground to take his place behind the broad leaves of a tall fern. Laying on the muddy ground Colin peered around the foliage to detect any movement up ahead. He saw ivy covered trees and more tall ferns. But nothing moved. If there was any enemy activity out there then it was certain that this noisy rain was concealing the sound of their movements.

Colin looked around at his comrades. They were all quiet and still. They were expecting to engage in a raging firefight at a second's notice. At Colin's far right his superior officer, Lieutenant Paul Yates was crouched down behind a tree. His laser rifle aimed towards the forest beyond.

Colin's personal communicator, a small oblong device with a keypad strapped to his wrist, transmitted the Lieutenant's voice. "McKenzie, see anything?"

"All clear on my end," Colin spoke into his communicator. But not seeing their enemy, the Brelac, did not mean that there was no threat. The Brelac were as stealthy as they were brutal.

Like most troopers Colin knew very little about the Brelac. The Brelac remained silent about themselves and their objectives. When they encroached upon the United Protectorate a year ago they attacked with the force of a tidal wave. The Protectorate was overwhelmed by the alien military force. Troopers fought back bravely on both land and in space. However, they were pitifully unprepared to deal with the Brelac's ferocity and advanced technology. The Protectorate suffered a year of crushing defeats. Seven star systems and twelve planets have been completely conquered by the Brelac. Many large cities with their gleaming towers and bustling populations were reduced to rubble. Now it would seem that Meridan was next on the Brelac's list. Unstopped they would eventually reach the center of the United Protectorate. The capital world of Maseklos Prime. Conquering that planet would seal the final downfall of the entire Protectorate.

Colin was startled when he felt someone touch his shoulder. He turned quickly, preparing to shoot. He was quickly relieved to see that it was trooper Ed Driscol who had crawled up behind him instead of a Brelac soldier.

"Take it easy, pal. It's just me," Driscol assured him.

Ed Driscol. Out of all the men in this platoon he was Colin's closest friend. He seemed to be near Colin whenever possible. Almost to the point of being a nuisance. Back at their main base, Helios, Driscol would eat with Colin, help him with weapons maintenance duties, and stick close to Colin in the off duty taverns and recreation halls. All the while denigrating the other members of the platoon. There were occasions when Colin felt that Driscol was keeping him under surveillance. It was no surprise to Colin that the man would be shadowing him even here during an impending battle.

"Let's move out," Lieutenant Yates called out through Colin's communicator. The same order would be heard by the rest of the platoon. The troopers began to advance cautiously among the trees and foliage.

The platoon approached their destination at the top of a small rocky hill. There was a dark rectangular aircraft resting at the bottom. It's nose was buried beneath a mound of soil. It's broad wings were sheared off. Bits of metallic wreckage littered the area. Thick billows of black smoke rose out from the ship's two damaged engine ports. This was a Brelac shuttle that had been shot down by a Protectorate fighter patrol. The platoon's mission was to investigate the crash site and see if any prisoners had survived or capture any cargo that was found to be reasonably intact.

Lieutenant Yates ordered the platoon to spread out and descend the hill. Colin wondered if anyone could have survived this crash. He kept his eyes on the shuttle. Alert for any movement. Lieutenant Yates raised his hand. The platoon stopped twenty feet away from the shuttle.

"A type three enemy shuttle," the Lieutenant stated after making a brief inspection.

A type three shuttle, as classified by Protectorate military intelligence, thought Colin. This craft only had one way to get inside. The main match located underneath the cabin. Since the platoon had no means of lifting a ship of this size they would have to create their own door.

"Bossar, Craven. Take demo charges and blow the hull," the Lieutenant ordered.

The two men rushed up to the ship. They took small packets from their weapons belts. The devices were magnetic, allowing the men to attach them to the ship's hull. They pressed small buttons on the side of the devises, then ran to rejoin the rest of the platoon.

"Hit the ground!" the Lieutenant cried out.

The platoon dove to the ground and covered their heads. The devises exploded. Their twin blasts were potent enough to rip a gaping hole into the side of the ship. Colin raised his head. He watched the smoke clear from the hole. There was still no sign of any Brelac.

"Usher, Sealman, Driscol, Craven. You're with me. The rest of you stay alert," the Lieutenant ordered.

Driscol placed his hand on Colin's shoulder. His grip was firm. "Time to go to work, pal. Looks like it's just you and me." Driscol rose up and joined the other three troopers as they escorted the Lieutenant over to the hole in the side of the ship. Colin felt relieved to be momentarily free of Driscol's imposing presence. He stood back up and watched Driscol and the other men. The Lieutenant was the first one to enter the ship. The others followed close behind him. Colin waited, keeping his rifle aimed at the ship.

After several tense seconds the Lieutenant relayed their status through Colin's communicator. "So far we're all clear. Still no Brelac. Everybody move in, but stay alert."

Colin complied with the order, as did the other men. He slowly advanced towards the ship. When he was close enough Colin was able to peer inside the hole in the ship's side and catch a glimpse of the shuttle's cargo. There were eight tall, white cylinders standing on what appeared to be a magnetic platform. The platform's strong magnetic field may have prevented the cylinders from falling over during the crash but it could not protect them from the damaging impact. Three of the cylinders were cracked. A bright yellow liquid had oozed out from the cracks and soaked the shuttle's floor.

"Wonder what's inside these containers?" Sealman asked.

"Beat's the hell outta me," replied the Lieutenant. "Some of them have been damaged by the crash. They're leaking this goop all over the place. If there are any Brelac here they might be in the cockpit."

"Let's hope they're dead," Usher's bitter comment. "What about these cylinders? Can you see what's inside?"

"No. Maybe we can break one of them open," the Lieutenant suggested. "Driscol, Craven. Give us a hand. Sealman, Usher. Go check out the cockpit."

Trooper Driscol placed his hand on Craven's shoulder. Craven suddenly screamed and fell to the floor. The instant Craven hit the floor his torso shattered. His plastic combat armor easily splintered into minute fragments. As did his head and arms.

The other men stood in horrified silence. They had just witnessed Craven's body being flash frozen. Transformed into a brittle state. And by his fellow trooper, Ed Driscol. The Lieutenant spun around and aimed his rifle at Driscol. Driscol delivered a forceful kick to the Lieutenant's chest and knocked him out of the ship. The Lieutenant fell onto his back against the soggy ground, creating a large splash of mud. He was uninjured by the fall and quickly aimed his rifle at Driscol a second time. In that brief instant Colin decided to take swift action. He aimed his rifle at the Lieutenant and opened fire. Four crimson bolts of laserfire easily ripped through the Lieutenant's body. The man emitted a painful grunt and lay motionless.

Colin was unsure if the Lieutenant was dead or simply wounded. Then again, he had no interest in the man's condition. All that mattered to Colin now was the mission that he shared with Driscol. It was their job to do everything in their power to prevent the United Protectorate from capturing the cylinders aboard this Brelac ship. And in order to accomplish that aim Colin was well prepared to use every power at his disposal.

A trooper standing near the Lieutenant raised his weapon.Colin moved faster, firing two laserbolts into the man's chest. The trooper quickly dropped to the ground. An assailant pounced on Colin from behind, wrapping a strong arm around his neck in a strangling hold. It would seem that Colin was helpless, providing that he was just an ordinary trooper. Colin was now forced to show the rest of the platoon the arcane level of deadly force that he was capable of using. Just as Driscol had performed against Craven.

Colin's entire body rapidly turned warm. A powerful surge of energy erupted from him. He and his assailant were bathed in a blue flash of light and an explosion of sparks. The heat that Colin felt had now become an intense fire on his back. He pulled himself free of the human burden that he carried. He turned to glimpse his handiwork. The trooper who foolishly tried to restrain him had now been transformed into a Human pyre. The flames were already being extinguished by the heavy rain. What would remain would be fragments of charred flesh and globs of melted plastic clinging to a blackened skeleton. Another person that Colin would forget the moment that he diverted his sight.

Trooper Sealman fired his laser rifle at Driscol. Three laserbolts burned into Driscol's chest. Driscol staggered back and raised his rifle at Sealman. His wounds slowed his movement, giving Sealman ample time to dive behind the collection of cylinders. A volley of laserbolts smoothly burned through several Cylinders but failed to hit Sealman. Two troopers outside the shuttle opened fire at Driscol. Multiple laserbolts penetrated his body. He thrashed in spasms of pain. With his last breath Driscol let out a defiant shout. He raised his weapon feebly, then stumbled and fell forward. His riddled body lay halfway out of the ship. His armor was soaked by his own blood.

Colin doubt that Driscol could have survived such that assault. There was no time to mourn the man who had clung to him like a faithful brother. The full burden of their mission now rested solely on Colin's shoulders. As well as the dilemma of his own survival through all this. Colin was surrounded by multiple hostile targets. Before he had a chance to act another trooper attacked him from behind. Colin felt a sharp and powerful impact jar the back of his head. He collapsed face down onto a mound of mud.

Colin turned his head to face his new assailant. A baby faced trooper stared wide eyed down at him. His rifle shook rapidly in his nervous hands. The barrel never leaving the direction of Colin's face. This frightened young man posed a small threat to Colin. He could kill this trooper as easily as he did the first.

Four blue streaks of fiery energy hit the trooper in his neck and head. The last shot easily split the top of the trooper's helmet and the head underneath. He fell to the ground. His blood and brains mingled with the rainwater and wet soil. Colin turned to the shuttle to see who had robbed him of his next kill. The shuttle's two Brelac pilots had chose this time to emerge and meet their enemies. The dark, scaley reptilian creatures stood nearly six feet tall. Their large lizard-like heads grinned with mouthfuls of long sharp teeth. The Brelac bore no eyes. Thick plates of scales covered the sides of their heads where the visual organs would have been. They had rounded bodies with boney plates covering their backs. Rows of long, sharp spikes ran along their sides. The Brelac's long tails thrashed about as they stormed from the ship. Their taloned hands clutched the typical Brelac field weapon. Long barreled plasma rifles. Weapons that were far more powerful than lasers. Their weapons belts strapped around their waists carried holstered pistols, Cylinder shaped grenades and bayonets with long gleaming blades.

The two Brelac immediately opened fire at any trooper that moved. The situation grew more chaotic as the screaming troopers scattered as they returned fire. The Brelac managed to gun down three troopers before a Human skillfully sent a laserbolt into one Brelac's head. The Brelac stumbled backward as his body absorbed the firepower from other Trooper's rifles. The Brelac's partner Shot and killed a trooper who was standing near Colin's head. As the man's dead body fell to the ground Colin saw that the Brelac was now training that plasma rifle in his direction. In this group of hostile, armed Humans the Brelac was not taking the time to distinguish between an enemy and an ally. Colin pointed his hand towards the Brelac. A blue flash and a stream of energy flew from Colin's land. It created a spray of sparks the moment it struck the Brelac. Colin's firepower was joined by dozens of laserbolts as the troopers concentrated their fire to bring the Brelac down.

Colin tried to stand up but he was again attacked. Colin was surprised to see that Lieutenant Yates had survived his wounds. Now he was standing over Colin, slamming the but of his laser rifle into Colin's face.

"I'm gonna bash your damn face in, freak!" The Lieutenant snarled at Colin.

He used the but of his rifle to rain down a series of painful blows on Colin's face. Colin felt the Lieutenant give him an occasional respite from the rifle but by giving him potent kicks into his legs and abdomen.

"Stupid freak! I'll kill you!" The Lieutenant continued his abuse on Colin.

Colin's face burned with pain. He could no longer feel his rifle in his hand. A mixture of blood and rainwater soaked his eyes. He lost sight of his attacker. He could only concentrate on the sensation of irrepressible pain that filled his head. He was totally helpless. Soon he lost consciousness.

CHAPTER 2

▼

Doctor Howard Fenlow, a young blond haired man in a white lab coat walked hastily through the busy corridors of Cerulean, a highly restricted military base. He was concerned that his black pants and slightly wrinkled grey shirt would be suitable enough for the important briefing that he was about to give. Fenlow had slept in and was running twenty minutes late. He had no time to make a better selection from his wardrobe. Fenlow's apartment was located in Navarone, the capital city here on the planet Maseklos Prime. It was less than two miles away from Cerulean. A convenient location, in Fenlow's opinion. That was one of the reasons why Fenlow chose to reside in Navarone. The city and this planet were the center of the United Protectorate. This planet was named after famed scientist and explorer, Leon Maseklos. Centuries ago his work helped to establish this planet as the first colony world for Humanity. From there mankind's influence would expand to become an empire that would encompass eighteen star systems and thirty two planets.

Fenlow approached the door to his laboratory. It was flanked by four armed troopers. They both stood silently while holding their laser rifles to their shoulders.

"I suppose everyone is inside waiting for me," Fenlow said to the guards.

"President Drennen was about to send us out to find you," a guard cheerlessly replied.

The door to the laboratory automatically slid open to admit Fenlow. His laboratory was a large room crowded by dozens of long tables holding various apparatus. There were dozens of test tubes and beakers filled with substances of different colors. Cabinets and shelves were lined up along the four walls. They were loaded with jars of chemicals, laboratory glassware and every scientific tool that Fenlow could lay his hands on. At the end of the room were two tall gleaming white cylinders.

There were already several other persons waiting here. One individual instantly caught Fenlow's eye. A middle aged woman in a black skirt and jacket. She had short brown hair and piercing green eyes. President Sandra Drennen of the Central Commission and Commander and Chief of the United Protectorate military forces did not appear to be pleased with having to wait for Fenlow to arrive at his leisure.

Fenlow admired Drennen for her accomplishments. Being elected president at the age of thirty nine, serving a second four year term. Now she was cursed with the monumental task of holding the Protectorate together during this war. Drennen was a highly intelligent and articulate person. Her personality was quiet and sensitive, yet she was strong enough to bear the torment of her people on her shoulders without losing her sanity. The Protectorate was holding it's own for the present time. But she knew that the Brelac were too powerful. And that the Protectorate would eventually lose. She would be willing to accept anything within reason to turn the war around in the Protectorate's favor.

Standing near Drennen was Secretary of Defense John Crane. A thin black man in a dark grey suit. He impatiently ran his fingers through his thinning black hair. There were also a few members of the Central Commission here. They were a part of the legislative body that helped Drennen govern the Protectorate. Joining Drennen and the Commissioners were several generals. Among them was Major General Verne Larkin. Dressed in his dark blue uniform with the band of medals on his left lapel. His dark blue cap with the gold eagle emblem sat proudly on his head.

Fenlow maintained a relationship with Larkin that could best be described as tolerance. Larkin directly stated that he considered Fenlow to be too arrogant and demanding for a person sitting out the war in the safety of a laboratory. He also distrusted Fenlow because he was employed by Carp technologies.

Carp was a large corporation owning laboratories and factories on seven planets throughout the protectorate. Carp was the leading producer of advanced electronics and bio-technology. Carp's motto was that it was committed holding the lead in the race for Human advancement. The company also produced a vast array of hardware for military use. The market for weapons lead to Carp being charged with reputedly selling arms to both sides during the bitter civil war seven years ago.

A movement evolved on several colony worlds to break away from the central government on Maseklos Prime. These planets intended to form their own ruling bodies. Many citizens did not agree with this quest for independence. But under the support of a political group calling itself, Vendetta, the movement was able to gain thousands of supporters. Growing weary of spouting demands to Maseklos Prime that would go unheeded Vendetta decided to take a drastic step. Under Vendetta's direction the rebel planets declaired their independence. And they intended to fight for their newly freed worlds.

A civil war erupted within the Protectorate. For two years vicious battles were fought in space and across each rebel planet. The cost was the loss of thousands of lives and untold property damage. But the end result was the eventual defeat of Vendetta's forces. Order was quickly restored throughout the Protectorate But Vendetta still remained active. Never losing sight of it's goal, the dissolution of the central government on Maseklos Prime.

After the war Vendetta's activities became more covert. The more fanatical members of the group waged a war of terror against the Protectorate. Their tactics included bombing vital government installations and assassinating key political and military figures. Their activities were gradually curtailed by the Protectorate's military intelligence internal security operations. Several of Vendetta's major resistance cells were eliminated. Their higher ranking leaders retreated into seclusion. Taking with them any hard evidence that may have linked Carp Technologies to Vendetta's activities during and after the war.

Seven years after the civil war General Larkin remained suspicious and hostile towards Carp Technologies. And that meant Fenlow as well. Fenlow paid little attention to Larkin's resentful attitude. He considered the man to be a small component within a larger machine. and Fenlow's rightful place was at the controls of this machine. Larkin would have to choke on the fact that he and his superiors needed the technologies and services that Fenlow and Carp provided.

There were two men in white lab coats standing near the group. One was a muscular young man with short cropped hair. He was Doctor Blair Van Doren, Fenlow's assistant. The other man was much older. At the age of sixty his face was mapped by thick wrinkles. His thinning white hair hung past his shoulders. His white lab coat made him appear as an undead specter in desperate search of a decent grave. He was Doctor Arnold Trevor. Another assistant to Fenlow. He was also a person who was regarded as the most ingenious computer scientist who had ever lived.

President Drenned voiced her displeasure with Fenlow. "I hope that we didn't tear you away from anything more important than this little meeting," her sarcastic rebuke.

"I apologize for my tardiness. I slept a bit too late this morning," Fenlow humbly stated. He expected to receive no more than a harsh scolding. Being a top scientist in the fields of electronics, bio-chemical engineering and genetics did earn Fenlow a certain level of leniency.

"As long as you're not too relaxed to sleep through the war," Larkin's stinging reply. Not intending to let Fenlow off the hook.

"We didn't come here to listen to any banter between you two,"President Drennen scolded. "I assembled this group here to learn if Doctor Fenlow has made any progress with this new project that I've heard so much about."

Fenlow proudly addressed the officials. "I've made great progress. I'll make this as brief and as clear as possible. As you know, we've learned very little about the Brelac during the start of the war. But as time moved on my research has revealed some startling facts about our mysterious enemies. Extensive examinations performed on several dead Brelac specimens has revealed that on a basic genetic level they are quite similar to Humans. If you remove their reptilian physiology they basically are Human. This has prodded me on to perform deeper research. I've picked apart every segment of the Brelac genetic sequence and discovered that they carry mutated genes. Examining a computer catalog of all known genetic anomalies I've learned that these genes are identical to the Pandora Simplex."

"The Pandora Simplex?" asked a surprised Drennen. "I haven't heard that mentioned since high school history class."

"Neither have I," Fenlow added. "A long forgotten disease that nearly wiped out the Human race. And if the Pandora Simplex is resurfacing after all these centuries then it's connection with the Brelac gives us a clue as to their origin. It's possible that the Brelac's point of origin could be Old Earth."

"Old Earth?" said Drennen. "That's not possible. History tells us that all life on that planet was destroyed by the virus. Then you're telling us that the Brelac are part Human."

"They're much more than part Human," Fenlow added. "I've run genetic scans on twenty dead specimens. My scans revealed that each one was genetically identical to the other. This suggests that the Brelac could employ an advanced in-vitro reploid technology to bolster their forces. In fact, their entire race could be comprised of reploids."

"That makes sense. They do have us vastly outnumbered," General Larkin pointed out. "They could artificially produce an army quicker than we can recruit and train our troops."

Fenlow continued. "The picture gets worse. Since the Brelac have such an advanced reploid technology we can assume that they can use it to reproduce other forms of life to suit their purpose. I bring to your attention the recent wave of terrorist activities that have plagued us of late."

"And it could not have happened at such a worse time," Drennen bitterly stated. "Military facilities being bombed, officers kidnaped or killed outright. Just last week there was that shooting spree on the street near the capital building. Twelve people dead, nine others wounded. And all these acts perpetrated by seemingly harmless citizens or military personnel. We think that Vendetta might pick this time to make a resurgence."

Fenlow nodded. "That's what I would have thought too. Until I received a report about an incident that took place on Core Three in the Hollander System. It seems that a police officer took several hostages inside of his own precinct. He later set off a bomb that destroyed the entire building. None of the hostages survived. Then I read reports of two other terrorist activities. The perpetrators were killed by police. Two of the terrorists involved in these incidents perfectly matched the physical description of the police officer on Core Three. I took the liberty of examining those two bodies. They were both identical. Even down to a genetic level."

Everyone in the room was astonished by Fenlow's revelation. And the dire ramifications that accompanied it.

"That's unthinkable," Drennen gasped fearfully. "You mean to say that the Brelac are somehow able to replicate Humans and use them against us. If that's true then they could strike us anywhere."

"There's another detail that could make the situation a whole lot worse," said Fenlow.

Larkin gave a frustrated moan. "You mean there's more? I came here in hope of hearing some good news. Instead you're giving us all bad."

"It's not entirely bad," Fenlow assured him. "Follow me and I'll explain." Fenlow lead the group over to the two white cylinders. "A week ago on the planet Meridan a Brelac shuttle was shot down near Helios base. A platoon of troopers investigated the shuttle and found a large group of cylinders like these. They are incubation units containing Human reploid specimens. During their investigation the troopers were attacked by two Reploids posing as members of the platoon. It was reported that one Reploid killed a trooper by freezing him to death."

Drennen was confused. "He froze the trooper to death?"

"With a touch of his hand," said Fenlow. "His combat armor and flesh were rendered so brittle that they shattered like glass. The second Reploid somehow generated enough energy to nearly incinerate one trooper. That Reploid was captured. The other one killed. During the melee the other cylinders in the shuttle were severely damaged. The Reploids that they contained did not survive. Only these two remained intact."

Fenlow went over to a table and brought back a small plastic dish. Inside the dish were several tiny transparent envelopes. Fenlow picked up one of the envelopes with great care and held it up for the group to see. The envelope contained a small, silvery disk shaped electronic component no bigger than a dime.

"This was one of the weapons that the Reploids used to kill the troopers. My assistant, Doctor Blair Van Doren aided me in performing the autopsy on the dead Reploid. I'll allow Blair to explain our findings."

Blair stepped forward. He nervously cleared his throat to address the group. "During our examination of every Brelac specimen we found components similar to these embedded deep within their brain's frontal and occipital lobes. Each Brelac had ten of these components embedded within it's brain. As you know, the Brelac have no physical eyes. These components are a form of psionic implants. Apparently they're designed to increase and focus the brain's level of psychic activity. This is how the Brelac are able to see. Psychic vision."

Larkin was underwhelmed by this information. "So they don't need bifocals. What does this have to do with those Reploids? And how can we use this to our advantage?"

"These components were taken from the slain Reploid," Blair explained. "They're more advanced than the standard Brelac implants that we've examined. They're designed to boost the brain's level of psionic power to a much higher degree. It's our theory that the Reploid's freezing ability was psychic in nature. A mental ability that was some how created by these implants."

"Imagine if every Reploid infiltrator had such a deadly psychic ability. Or every Brelac soldier," Fenlow said. "The power to read minds from a distance for vital information. As well as the power to kill in a number of paranormal ways. All the other Reploids in that shuttle had these same implants."

The distressed look on Drennen's face revealed that she was not pleased with this dire report. "It would be impossible to fight against such a covert threat backed by this technology. Is there any way that we can use these implants for our own troopers?"

"I'm afraid that these implants are useless to us," Fenlow regretfully admitted. "We've already tested them on chimpanzees. The sudden massive increase of psionic energy quickly burned out their entire nervous systems. But the Reploids apparently have a special cellular adaptation that allows them to completely regenerate damaged nervous tissue. And at a rapid pace. This would effectively counteract any damage inflicted by the psionic energy surge. We're studying tissue samples taken from the live Reploid that's in our custody. We're working to isolate the gene that enables his neural regeneration. But in the meantime we can put him and these other two to work for us."

"Put these creatures to work for us?" said a skeptical Larkin. "Weren't they created to fight against us? What do you plan to do, bribe them?"

"No. Reprogram them," Fenlow proudly returned. "We've discovered that the Reploid's brains also contain six implants that we call access memory chips. Apparently the Reploid's programmed memories are stored in these chips and downloaded into their brains as they first awaken. Since these two arrived to us in an unconscious state I believe that their programs have not been downloaded. This gives us the opportunity to program the Reploids to serve us instead of the Brelac."

"And what about the captured Reploid that was already functioning?" asked Drennen.

Blair explained, "That Reploid is under sedation. I can surgically remove the memory chips from it's brain. Along with these two. Doctor Trevor can delete the chips data and enter his own programs for the Reploids."

With a stiff stride Doctor Trevor stepped forward and gave his explanation. "It won't be an easy job. In order for the Reploids to blend in as one of us the Brelac had to program them with every aspect of an intelligent Human mind. They simulate emotions. They have different attitudes and memories of past experiences. Each Reploid is a unique individual. I believe that I can reproduce these highly intricate programs. I can reproduce every aspect of a normal mature Human mind."

Fenlow explained further. "We believe that the Brelac abduct Human victims and replicate them. Somehow they copy as much data as they can from the minds of the Human originals and program the data into the Reploids. Along with their programmed instructions to act against us. The originals, having served their purpose, are probably destroyed."

Drennen closed her eyes and shook her head in disgust. "Sounds horrible."

Remaining silent up to this point Secretary Crane decided to add his comment. "Sounds dangerous. This whole idea of trying to use these walking weapons could blow up in our faces."

"It can't hurt to try," Larkin's comment. "We could certainly use anything to help turn the tide of this war. God knows that we're sending everything we've got against the Brelac and we're still on a crumbling defensive. I'm at the point where I'm considering sending out exploding chain letters. But if these Reploids are going to be any good to us then we'll definitely need more than just three. Is it possible that we can produce our own Reploids? As well as these psionic implants?"

"At the present Carp's research into advanced cloning in limited," Fenlow's reply. "We can only produce cloned children through surrogate host mothers. These creatures are created through an advanced in-vitro process that we have yet to understand. Inside these cylinders the Reploids are immersed in a highly concentrated nutrient liquid. I've analyzed the liquid and found that it triggers rapid cell growth and nurtures the Reploids throughout their entire development. It's possible that the Brelac can produce these creatures in a matter of days. As for the psionic implants, we're just beginning to understand how they work. It will be some time before we can reproduce this technology. The research section back at Carp's main starbase has put our top people to work on both problems. I'm confident that a breakthrough will come in a few months."

"And at what cost?" inquired Larkin.

Larkin was still resentful of what he perceived as Carp's profiteering off of the war. Fenlow had ventured into this turbulent subject with him on several occasions. "The cost for this project will be determined when Secretary Crane negotiates with our board of directors. Our costs for manpower and materials for our research and development demand that we be fairly compensated. Even so, Carp is fully committed to the United Protectorate's war effort."

Crane sought to defuse any tension that would arise between Fenlow and Larkin. "We don't doubt your company's commitment to our cause. And the General would have to admit that Carp has made several significant discoveries that have placed us on better ground with the Brelac."

Larkin was forced to grudgingly relent on the point. "Perhaps Carp has been useful in reproducing captured Brelac technology for our use. Some of which I'm still getting used to. Like this hyperspace technology that you introduced a few months ago. But I'd still like to see Carp try to be a little charitable during these tough times."

"We'll have time to bicker when things improve," Drennen declared. "Right now I have to decide on whether to approve this project or not. And I honestly like what I've been hearing. Are there any objections?"

Crane admitted his fears. "I'm still leery of the idea of experimenting with enemy Reploids armed with dangerous abilities. Especially here on our home world. Something could go wrong. Perhaps it would be safer to transport them to Starbase Lodestar until all tests are complete. Located out in deep space it's the ideal facility to develop this project."

Drennen agreed with Crane's suggestion. "Any objections to the idea, Doctor?"

"I can live with it," said Fenlow.

There were no voices of objection for the project.

"Then it's settled," Drenned stated. "I just hope that this will be worth all the time and effort involved."

Larkin took a final glance at the two cylinders. "If there's anything nothing else then I'd like to get back to the war."

"Have the Reploids transported to Lodestar as soon as possible, Doctor," Drenned ordered. "Keep me posted about their development." She turned to the door. Larkin was already rushing out of the room. The other Generals and Commissioners were behind him.

Fenlow returned to his apartment building late in the evening. He approached his apartment door and entered his personal identification number on a small keypad at the right. The door slid open with a faint hiss. Fenlow's living room was small with modest furnishings. In the center of the room the brown easy chair sat across from the small sofa. Both items perfectly matched the brown carpeting. The large thin television screen looked like a dark canvas as it was propped up on a table in front of the chair.

On the left side of the room was Fenlow's work table. It held several beakers and test tubes filled with chemical solutions. There was also a computer sitting next to a large stack of papers. This was where Fenlow worked on future projects in his spare time. There was a chorus of loud beeps coming from the computer. It had recorded a subspace message received through it's uplink modem. Fenlow hoped that it would be a short message. He sat down in front of the computer's black monitor and pressed a key to run the message.

The image of a blond haired, middle aged man in a dark suit appeared on the monitor. He was sitting behind a desk with his hands folded in front of him. Fenlow suspected that the message might be from this man. Walter Carnaby, the

Chief Executive Officer of Carp Technologies. As well as Fenlow's immediate boss.

Walter Carnaby was a man capable of being an alluring, smooth talker. He was skilled in the art of selling unpopular concepts, or sidestepping unpleasant issues. When necessary Carnaby could easily adopt a more aggressive mode of behavior. He was known to be like a swarm of boulders in an avalanche. Not stopping for any smaller force until he reached his goal. The smaller force in his way was often crushed and forgotten.

Under Carnaby's leadership Carp Technologies had become the largest corporation in the United Protectorate. He initiated several successful takeovers of smaller rival companies. Carp absorbed their key personnel to strengthen it's position as a corporate leader. Carnaby was showered with continuous accolades from the business establishment. Still, Fenlow often wondered if the man was indeed worth the eighty million dollars in salary and stock options that the company paid him. But Fenlow was a scientist, devoting little interest in board room moving and shaking. His only interest was conducting research and development. As long as Carnaby continued to foot the bill.

Carnaby's greeting was buoyant. "Howard. I was trying to contact you earlier, but I guess you were out. I just met with the board of directors. We're concerned about the Brelac stepping up their aggression. Protectorate forces are falling back on several fronts. This means that we're forced to advance with our own plans. I'm making the preparations for Operation Broadaxe. I need you to step up your efforts in the field so that the plan can go through. I'll be expecting a report from you soon. Perhaps we can trade good news."

The monitor went black at the end of the message. Fenlow gave a tired sigh. Advance Operation Broadaxe so soon? Was Carnaby insane? Perhaps the Brelac were starting to worry Carnaby and the other stiff suits back at Carp's starbase headquarters. Whatever the reason it was Fenlow's job to help insure that Operation Broadaxe was a huge success. But advancing the plan now would force him to take some extremely drastic measures. But not now. At the moment Fenlow was concerned about eating the slice of lemon pound cake in his refrigerator while finishing the electronic designs that he was working on at his computer. Fenlow headed for his kitchen doorway.

CHAPTER 3

▼

Out in the desert, on the planet Talos, Fenlow was not enjoying the ride on his glider cycle. The wheelless motorcycle styled vehicle moved too rapidly for him to gain a smooth level of control. Plus it churned up huge clouds of dust in it's wake as it glided above the ground. The cycle's speed varied from fast to slow as Fenlow struggled to maintain control of the vehicle. His main irritation was that he did not need the dust clouds bringing premature attention to his presence out here.

Fenlow stopped the cycle and peered through the long ranged binoculars hanging around his neck. He made a quick visual scan of the north and saw nothing of importance. Just a bleak scene composed of sand, rocks and hills. A view to the east displayed the same image. Then looking to the south revealed moving figures in the distance. They were a mile away from his position. A small group composed of Humans and Brelac. The window of opportunity that Fenlow was searching for was now wide open before him. He drove his glider cycle towards his goal at top speed.

Drawing rapidly closer to the target area Fenlow could see the group more clearly without the aid of his binoculars. Two troopers were standing near what appeared to be a small jet. It was a transport shuttle. The troopers had rifles trained on five Brelac soldiers who were kneeling on the ground with their hands folded behind their heads. It was a proud achievement when Protectorate troopers could take Brelac prisoners. There was a third trooper laying against the shuttle. He had a bleeding abdominal wound. His combat armor's breastplate was removed to expose a blood soaked shirt tied crudely around his torso.

Fenlow stopped his cycle a few feet from the group. As Fenlow expected, at least one trooper defensively aimed his rifle towards him. Fenlow cheerfully introduced himself. "Good afternoon. My name is Howard Fenlow. I'm a doctor. What happened here?"

The trooper aiming his rifle spoke up. "Our squad set up an ambush in the hills for a gang of these bastards. We killed three of them before the group scattered and ran off. Fortunately we were able to capture these five. The other members of our squad are out trying to capture or take down the rest of them."

"You say you're a doctor?" asked the other trooper. "Baker here could use your help."

Fenlow quickly dismounted his cycle and went over to the injured trooper. The man was unconscious. Fenlow examined his wound. "This is serious. Your friend need needs surgury as soon as possible if he's to survive. In the meantime I've got some medical supplies in my cycle's storage compartment. I can try to stop his bleeding and keep him stable until we get him to a proper medical facility."

"Do what you can for him, Doc," the trooper said.

Fenlow went to the back of his cycle and opened the storage compartment.

The trooper pointing the rifle kept his gaze locked on Fenlow. "Just what are you doing out here, Doc?"

"I was part of a medical team being transferred to Norcross. Our ship was forced down by Brelac fighters. We survived the crash and was forced to scatter when Brelac troops started to chase us. They're relentless monsters. I was damn lucky to shake them off. I hope your squad returns soon. If the Brelac should pick up my trail then we'll definitely need some extra firepower. Which way did they go?"

The trooper turned his head to a group of hills in the horizon. "Over that way. It shouldn't take them long to track down the rest of the Brelac."

It only took a second for Fenlow to take the laser pistol that he had hidden in the cycle's storage compartment and squeeze off a shot at the back of the trooper's head. The laser bolt burned a large hole through the top portion of the man's head and killed him instantly. The second trooper looked on in shocked disbelief. The lifeless body of his partner dropped limply to the ground. Fenlow quickly fired four laser bolts into the second trooper's chest. The trooper stumbled back and fell. He lay motionless, quite dead.

Fenlow turned and approached the five Brelac prisoners. A smug grin formed on his face. He held his pistol out in front of him. He casually let the weapon slide out of his hand and drop to the ground. Then he addressed the Brelac.

"Let me introduce myself again. I'm Doctor Howard Fenlow. I was wondering if you could help me make a house call."

CHAPTER 4

▼

"I'll kill you!"

The enraged voice of Lieutenant Yates echoed through Colin's mind, repeating those harsh words over and over. In his mind he could clearly visualize the man standing over him. Torrents of rain drenching both their bodies as the Lieutenant sadistically pounded him with the butt of that laser rifle. Colin could see his own crimson blood streaming from his nose and quickly mixing with the rain water that soaked his face. But under the impact of the Lieutenant's every blow Colin felt no pain. He could not feel the cold rainwater that drenched his body. He could only hear the threatening words growled by an inflamed Lieutenant Yates.

"I'll kill you!" Yate's rifle butt delivered a crushing blow onto Colin's nose. "I'll kill you!" Colin saw his body convulse under the impact. The Lieutenant shouted at him again. "I'll kill you! I'll kill you! I'll kill you!"ending each threat with a hard blow from his rifle butt. All the while Colin could feel no sensation.

Then the deafening sound of an explosion filled Colin's ears. He felt a powerful force shove his body forward. A second later he felt a sharp pain spread along his back. He opened his eyes. He was not on the rainy planet, Meridan. He was not being mercilessly beaten by Lieutenant Yates. Colin was immediately shocked to see that he had awoke inside of a dark, oblong cylinder. A steady stream of air rushed into his face. The right side of the cylinder was completely shattered. The cylinder was thickly lined with a dark plastic cushion that would have held Colin's body firmly in place. But the upper portion of the cushion was ripped open. He could barely see it in these dimly lit surroundings but it was there. Shreds of the outer covering flapping in his face.

Colin was able to conclude that this plastic was once an airbag. Now the two questions running through his mind were how did it become damaged and how did he arrive within it's embrace?

Seeking the answers to these questions would have to wait. For now Colin's priority was to free himself from this damaged cylinder. He was able to easily push away it's shattered lid. His legs were numb but strong enough to support his weight. As Colin tried to move away from the tube he felt a sharp pain in his left arm. There was a plastic transparent tube inserted into his arm. The other end of the tube led back to a small grey box mounted on the inside of the cylinder.

Colin was curious about this tube's purpose and who placed it there. More questions that he would have to answer at a later time. Right now Colin would be content with simply removing this tubing from his arm. There was a brief sting when he yanked the tube out of his arm. He was amazed that he did not feel any greater pain when he examined the long needle that was attached to the tube.

When Colin emerged from the cylinder he was now able to examine his apparel. He found himself dressed in loose fitting blue coveralls and black boots. Not the cumbersome combat armor and brown uniform that he was familiar with. Being unarmed was no surprise to him. Whoever confined him to that cylinder did not intend to allow him the freedom of being a potential threat.

There were two other cylinders next to the one that Colin emerged from. He could not see how the three cylinders were attached to the wall. However, the large bulge on the wall behind them and the jagged crack running along it's metallic surface were not hard to miss. There were also large splinters of twisted metal protruding from the wall. One of these sharp fragments tore through the left side of Colin's cylinder. This explained the damage. As well as the sudden pain that he felt. He was thankful that the fragment did not penetrate a few more inches to the right. He could picture himself being skewered and dying slowly in intense pain.

Colin suspected what these other two cylinders might contain. The force that damaged his cylinder also seriously cracked these two. He was able to open the lid on one to reveal an unconscious young woman. She appeared to be Colin's height, six feet tall. Her long black hair obscured her face and hung down past her shoulders. She was also wearing blue coveralls similar to Colin's. Colin spotted a plastic tube inserted into the woman's arm. Whatever the tube's purpose Colin imagined that the woman would be grateful if he removed it. He yanked the tube out of her arm, then shook her. The woman did not wake. Colin shook her again but she remained unconscious. He concluded that he would get nowhere with her and decided to see what was in the next cylinder.

The second cylinder opened just as easily. Inside this one was a young man with short cropped blond hair. He had a youthful face, appearing to be in his late teens or early twenties. The young man was shorter than Colin and the female. Colin estimated his height to be five feet, four inches. There was also a mysterious tube inserted into his arm as well. Colin removed the tube and tried to rouse the youth. Like the woman the young man remained in a deep slumber and could not be awakened.

Colin decided not to wait until these two revived on their own. He would go beyond this storage room to find the answers that he sought. He approached the door. Whatever force damaged this room also affected the door. It had slid halfway open. Beyond the door Colin could clearly hear a loud wailing noise. An alarm of some sort, he thought. He also heard the sounds of panicked shouting and running footsteps.

Colin left the storage room and entered a small corridor that was filled with smoke. The column of dim lights along both walls provided little aid for his vision. He wondered where this corridor led to or from, then decided to head to the right. Towards the sounds of shouting. He felt that he would have a better chance of finding someone by heading into the heart of whatever chaos he was in.

Colin was surprised when a man suddenly rushed up to him through the smoke. The man was dressed in a dark blue uniform. There were gold insignias of Captain's bars on his shoulders. There was a gun belt strapped to his waist. Colin recognized this as a pilot's uniform. The man instantly halted in his tracks when he saw Colin. "Who the hell are you?" he rudely demanded.

Colin hesitated to reply. He felt intimidated by this man's hostile demeanor.

"This ship is restricted to authorized personnel only!" the man snapped at Colin. He reached for the weapon holstered at his right side.

Colin instantly interpreted this action as a threat. He swiftly hurled his fist into the man's face. The man staggered back into the wall. Colin chose not to follow up on his attack. Instead he darted past the man and headed down the corridor.

"Intruder alert! Intruder on board!" Colin heard the man's voice cry out.

Colin concluded that if he were aboard a ship then he would have a limited area in which to run. He had already encountered one hostile crew member. Undoubtably there would be more. He had to either find a place to hide or get off this ship.

Colin came to a large open ramp. It would appear that this ship was still on the ground. This came as a relief to Colin. His escape could now be easier, depending on what was waiting for him at the bottom of the ramp. Colin's bid for freedom was suddenly cut short when he felt someone grab him from behind. Obviously the man that Colin had assaulted in the corridor. The man's weight forced Colin down. He wrapped his arm tightly around Colin's neck. His hand gripped Colin's right arm. Colin desperately tried to wrestle free but he was helpless against the man's strength. All he could hope to do was roll down the ramp with his attacker clinging to his back.

Taking a quick glimpse of his new surroundings Colin saw that he was in a large airbay. It appeared to be located underground. Rows of blinding white lights were mounded high along the rock walls. Dozens of triangular shaped fighter craft were parked on both side of the painted runway. The large wedge shaped vessel that Colin emerged from bore a huge mass of flaming wreckage imbedded in the side of it's hull. That explained the source of the smoke, Colin thought. Several troopers were scrambling left and right. A few watched to watch the struggle between Colin and his assailant. Three troopers broke away from the crowd and rushed over to the ramp. They grabbed Colin's arms and pulled him up. Colin found himself being forcefully and swiftly dragged along until he was slammed face first against the hard stone wall.

"Who are you?" a loud and angry voice shouted into Colin's ear.

Colin did not respond. The men punished him by puling him back and slamming him into the wall a second time. Intense agony penetrated Colin's face.

"Who are you?" How did you get into this base?" the bellowing voice demanded.

Colin answered to avoid absorbing any more painful abuse. "I'm Sergeant Colin McKenzie. Assigned to platoon Three, Six, Seven. Fourteenth Combat Division."

"I'm not impressed, Sergeant!" the voice snarled back. "I'd be more impressed if you tell me how you got aboard a ship that's restricted to authorized personnel only!"

"That's what I'd like to know. I just woke up there," Colin desperately replied.

The men pulled Colin back and slammed him into the wall a third time. All other sensations throughout Colin's body were instantly overshadowed by the pain in his face. He expected to hear the trooper's impatient voice interrogating him again. Instead he heard a different voice forcefully shouting out the command, "Stop!"

Colin turned his head and saw a young man casually dressed in blue denim jeans, a red sweater and white sneakers. He was accompanied by an old man dressed in a grey suit.

"Let him go," the young man's stern command to the troopers.

"Let him go? The man's under arrest for trespassing aboard a high security vessel," one of the troopers protested.

"That won't be necessary. He's with us," the old man said. "He's part of our cargo. I can personally vouch for him."

The troopers hesitated for a moment. Then they released Colin.

Colin rubbed his nose. It was still sore after being slammed into the wall.

The young man approached Colin. "Who are you again?" he inquired.

"I already told you. I'm Sergeant Colin McKenzie. Platoon three, six, seven. Fourteenth Combat Division." Was Colin's impatient reply. "Who the hell are you?"

"I'm Doctor Blair Van Doren," the young man answered. "My associate here is Doctor Arnold Trevor. He's a computer specialist. How do you feel? Are you ok?"

Colin's patience was wearing thinner with each second. "I'm not ok," he groused. I just had my face imprinted against the wall."

"I apologize for that," Doctor Trevor humbly replied. "This ship is under a high security restriction. I'm afraid that Captain Gains here overreacted to your unexpected presence. It would help if you could tell us how you arrived here."

"I just woke up inside this cylinder. I was having this dream, then I felt something hit me. That's when I woke up. The cylinder was pretty badly damaged."

Doctor Trevor gave a nod. "Sounds logical. Earlier there was an accident here. A heavily damaged ship crashed into ours. The impact of the crash must have damaged your containment cylinder and awakened you."

Colin was satisfied with that explanation. That was one question among many that he needed to be answered.

"What about the others?" asked Blair.

"Those other two? They were both unconscious. I tried to wake them but they were too far out of it," said Colin.

Blair and Doctor Trevor both rushed past Colin and up the ramp into the ship. Still needing answers from these two Colin quickly followed close behind them.

Inside the storage room Blair examined the cylinder that contained the sleeping female. "Her intravenous tube has been removed," Blair exclaimed in shock. Holding out the limply dangling tubing.

"I know. I took it out," Colin's casual reply.

Blair examined the cylinder containing the young man. "Did you remove this one as well?" asked an angered Blair.

"I removed it. Just like I took out mine," Colin freely admitted. "I wasn't sure as to what purpose it served."

With a one of annoyance Blair explained, "These tubes are part of a timed intravenous unit installed within these cylinders. The units are supposed to pump a dosage of sedatives into their recipients every two hours."

The woman emitted a faint moan. Her head swivelled left to right. Then the youth stiffly lifted his arms.

"It's a moot point now," Doctor Trevor commented. "They're both waking up."

"What's the purpose behind keeping us sedated?" asked Colin.

"To ensure your safety during our trip to Lodestar," Doctor Trevor answered. "Unfortunately an increased Brelac presence in this sector forced us to seek refuge here in Scorpis, a small base on the Planet Voran. But it appears that even here we're shadowed by the threat of the Brelac."

The woman opened her eyes and looked about. She seemed to be confused about her surroundings. "What happened? Where am I?"

"You're aboard a cargo cruiser presently resting within a small base on the planet Voran," Doctor Trevor told her.

Blair helped the youth out of his cylinder while Doctor Trevor assisted the stiffly moving female.

"How do you both feel?" Doctor Trevor asked.

The woman answered first. "I'm ok. I just feel a little dizzy."

"Me too," the youth answered. "How long have I been out?"

"Only a few days," said Blair. "But we didn't expect you three to awaken so soon. Does any of you remember anything before you came here?"

The young man calmly explained, "I remember being on duty at Helios, a communications outpost on Meridan. Then the Brelac attacked."

"What was your job?" Blair inquired.

"Trooper Kelly Kirby, Technical Master first Class. I was repairing a computer terminal in the central command center. I must have been shot because I don't remember anything beyond that."

"Same here," said the woman with surprise. "All I remember was that I was coming back from a mission. And that's it."

"What was the mission?" Blair inquired.

She looked confused as she replied, "I don't remember. All I know was that I was in a fighter. I'm a pilot. Captain Diane Christy. Credited with two hundred and thirty confirmed enemy kills.:

"Quite an impressive score," Doctor Trevor's complement. "I'm sorry that we haven't been properly introduced. My name is Doctor Arnold Trevor. I'm a computer scientist. My young friend here is Doctor Blair Van Doren. The reason that you are all here is that you were seriously injured while on duty. You were each hanging close to death. Our only chance to save you was to conduce a series of experimental operations. These operations not only saved your lives but endowed you with certain paranormal abilities. We were planning to take you to Lodestar to recuperate and undergo special training. You each possess a different power that we hope to use against the Brelac. You are a new squad composed of specially modified troopers. Silencers Squad. Depending on how effective you are against the Brelac will determine if more of your kind will be created."

Diane and Kelly took a few minutes for their minds to absorb everything that was explained to them. Colin held Doctor Trevor's story under scrutiny. "Some of what you're saying makes sense so far. But why take us all the way to Lodestar?"

"As a security measure," said Doctor Trevor. "You three are part of a highly sensitive military project. It's success is all too important."

Diane voiced her apprehensions. "Only three of us? You're not going to send us out on any suicide missions, are you?"

Kelly also had his questions. "What kind of paranormal abilities are you talking about? And how do we use them? I don't feel anything out of the ordinary."

"You will when the proper time comes," Doctor Trevor told him.

Captain Gains entered the room and quickly approached Blair and doctor Trevor. "I've inspected the hull and used the ship's sensors to run a full diagnostic. We were lucky. That crash only breached a small section of our hull. But we can easily seal this entire section off during our flight. And all of the ship's systems check out ok. Also the flight controllers just told me that their scanners show that enemy traffic around the planet has abated. But this might not last very long."

"Then we'd better leave now," said Doctor Trevor.

Blair pointed to Colin, Diane and Kelly. "What about them?"

"The hull breach is forcing us to seal off this entire section. And our friends here are already awake so we have no choice but to have them sit up front with us," Doctor Trevor's explanation.

The group followed captain Gains out of the room and up a short flight of steps at the end of the left corridor. It was here on the next deck that they assembled in the small passenger section located behind the cockpit. Captain Gains headed for the cockpit and securely strapped himself to his pilot's chair. Blair assisted Colin with his thick safety harness. He went on to help Diane and Kelly, who were seated across from Colin. After Blair made sure that the three were strapped in he sat down next to Doctor Trevor, who was seated up front.

The loud whine of the ramp being raised filled the ship's interior. Once the ship was sealed tightly the whine was replaced by the powerful thrum and vibrations that were generated by the ship's engines.

"The wreckage is cleared away," Captain Gains announced. "Now sealing off lower deck."

Colin could clearly see into the cockpit and through the panoramic forward window. The ship rose into the air and slowly headed for the runway. It turned and faced the gaping exit to this subterranean base. Then it sped out of the airbay.

The ship kept low to the ground while Protectorate and Brelac fighters continued to battle overhead. Captain Gains explained his plan to try to keep low to the ground and hopefully fly under the skirmish until the ship cleared the area. Then he would pilot the ship safely up into space.

It would appear that the damage inflicted upon the ship back at Scorpis was not hampering it's performance. Now Colin hoped that Captain Gains tactic to escape the Brelac's attention would work. The ship traveled above the rocky hilltops for five minutes without incident. Colin was starting to slowly feel relieved. Confident that they would soon arrive safely at Lodestar. Then a violent tremor rocked the ship.

"We've got trouble," Captain Gains reported. "We were hit by enemy fire. Shields holding. No internal damage. Scanners have picked up four Brelac fighters on our tail. I'll try to outrun them."

It would appear that their attempted escape would not go unnoticed by the Brelac. Colin could not imagine this small ship surviving an encounter with four Brelac fighters. The fear in his mind visualized this ship as an instant death trap. And he would have a front row seat to witness his own destruction.

Diane unstrapped herself and rushed into the cockpit. Engrossed with his piloting Captain Gains failed to notice her approach.

"Maybe I'd better take over, Diane told him. "I can handle our friends outside."

Switching pilots at such a crucial time would not make Colin feel secure. "Sit down, lady. Let the man do his job," his angry voice cried out.

The ship made a sharp turn and headed into the sky. Captain Gains thrust the ship into wild zig zagging maneuvers to avoid the enemy's fire. Unfortunately this would not be enough. Another violent tremor rocked the ship. This one was far louder than the first.

"Engine trouble!" Captain Gains cried out. "Hang on back there. This might be a little rough!"

Diane ran back to her seat. The ship began to descend rapidly. It would appear that Captain Gains was barely able to control it's flight. Colin watched him jerk the twin control sticks back sharply but gaining little response. The ship plowed into the ground and skidded for a short distance. Then it's momentum came to an abrupt halt when it crashed into the base of a large hill. This ship's journey was now over.

Colin's body throbbed with pain. He was fortunate that he was strapped in his seat instead of being bounced against the bulkhead. He was amazed to see that the ship did not explode after enduring the massive impact of the crash. He looked over at Diane and Kelly. They were both slumped over in an unconscious state. Colin wondered if Blair, Doctor Trevor and Captain Gains were injured. Captain Gains was not moving. The forward window had shattered. Large splinters of plastiglass littered the cockpit. Now a black acrid smoke started to fill the ship. A fire would pose a serious threat.

Colin started to unbuckle his safety belt when he glanced through the broken out forward window and saw a mob of ragged figures rushing through. They were men and women dressed in dirty robes and capes. Colin glimpsed a few men clad only in short loincloths. He was not concerned with their attire. He was wondering why this screaming mob was intruding upon the ship. And what threat they would pose.

One of the men headed swiftly towards Colin. He was tall and muscular. His uncombed black hair grew far past his shoulders. He was wearing a pair of dirty ragged shorts and a hooded robe both made from the scaley hide of some reptilian creature. His massive fist dashed into Colin's face. Colin closed his eyes as intense pain flooded his head. He did not register the sensation of falling back against his seat. He lost consciousness, shrouded in darkness.

CHAPTER 5

▼

The two Brelac guards dragged Doctor Fenlow arm in arm through the dark corridors of their base. After freeing the five Brelac prisoners back on Talos they in turn took Fenlow prisoner and transported him here. He was completely in the dark as to which planet and base he was on. But names and locations were unimportant. As long as he was here. Fenlow had a special purpose in mind.

Fenlow expected to be subjected to some form of physical abuse the moment he arrived here. He firmly stated his motives and suspected that the Brelac went as easy on him as they could during his interrogation. If you can consider repeated blows with electrically charged metal rods and being slammed against a stone wall soft treatment. Fenlow endured his punishment with dignity. Never losing sight of his mission. During his torments Fenlow reminded himself that if he survived and got what he wanted from the Brelac then his suffering would be well worth it.

The guards took Fenlow through a set of twin doors. He now found himself in a cold and dark ballroom. Several Brelac were seated behind a long banquet table. There was a large meal laid out before them. Sides of roast beef, turkeys, legs of lamb, fresh fruit and vegetable salads. The diners were heartily eating and drinking their fill. They gulped down large quantities of beer and wine. There were other tables situated throughout the room with more Brelac eating and drinking heavily. Others were standing around the dark and featureless room holding conversations.

All activity in the ballroom ceased. One of the Brelac sitting behind the banquet table belched in a deep raspy voice, then acknowledged Fenlow."What do we have here?" the Brelac buoyantly inquired. "Looks like an unexpected dinner guest. Sorry, this party's by invitation only."

"My invitation was probably lost in the mail," Fenlow replied. "Things are pretty hectic these days with the war going on."

To punish Fenlow for his flippant response the guard on his left quickly slapped his face with a crack that was as painful as it was loud. With Fenlow silenced the guard issued his report.

"The prisoner was aboard a Protectorate shuttle with five of our soldiers. They have all stated that they were being held prisoner on the planet Talos by Protectorate troopers. Then this man came onto the scene. He killed two of his own comrades and turned his weapon over to our soldiers. They killed a third trooper, then escaped in the shuttle. The prisoner continuously insisted on being brought to see our superiors. Important business, he stated. Says his name is Doctor Howard Fenlow. Insists that you would know him."

The Brelac left his seat and walked over to give Fenlow a closer inspection. He stopped inches away from Fenlow and scanned him from head to foot. "Are you sure he's not wired to blow? Or maybe rigged up with some kind of a spy device to transmit everything he sees and hears."

The guard replied, "We've ruled out those possibilities, sir. Once he arrived the prisoner was strip searched and examined with several different probes inside and out. We found no hidden devices of any kind."

"I can vouch for that," added Fenlow. "My back is still sore from bending over for so long."

"You came here willingly?" asked the Brelac. "Even killed three of your own to do it?"

"I had to make an unfortunate choice. But it was necessary in order for me to be here," Fenlow explained. "It was vital that I meet with someone of a rank higher than that of my two chaperones here."

The Brelac began to laugh boisterously. Fenlow hoped that this was a positive sign. He knew that these creatures were as unpredictable as they were vicious. The laughter could mean that this Brelac was intending to embrace a new friend. Or he could be contemplating a lingering method of executing a Human prisoner as after dinner entertainment.

"So you're the Great Doctor Fenlow," said the Brelac. "One of the first traitors in the brief history of this war. We finally meet."

Fenlow was quick to voice his indignity to that unsavory title. "I find the word, traitor to be a little too malignant to suit my purpose. I'd like to think of myself as an entrepreneur."

The Brelac laughed again. "Traitor, entrepreneur. It's all the same to me. The point is that you're here. Now the question is why are you here?"

"I'm here to speak to Bane Mariner. I have a proposition for him."

"You are addressing Governor General Bane Mariner. Supreme Commander of the Brelac Empire. And I hope that your proposition is worth my time."

"It is," Fenlow assured him. "What I'm about to propose will greatly benefit both you and my company."

"Carp Technologies," Mariner stated with a chuckle. "I admire your company. Playing both sides of the war for their own benefit. All the while maintaining the facade of a benevolent corporation serving your little corner of the universe. I wonder what your people would say if they knew that you and your company were working with us to create the Reploid menace? Including the advanced Reploids with psionic powers."

Fenlow had unfortunate news that he was sure that Mariner would not like. "I'm afraid that the Reploid program has been discontinued for the present time. Especially the advanced Reploids. En-route to Helios on the planet Meridan one of your shuttles carrying several advanced Reploid units was shot down by Protectorate forces. Three Reploids were captured by the military. Carp considered this to be a threat to company security and decided to halt the project."

Fenlow was withholding the fact that he had recommended halting the Reploid project. Aided by Carp's resources Fenlow produced the Reploids at one of Carp's deep space laboratories. Fenlow notified his Brelac contact on a secured channel when each shipment of Reploids would be due for delivery. A cargo shuttle would deliver the Reploids to a designated rendevous point in space.

Curious about the Brelac's vision without the use of physical eyes Fenlow asked to examine their psionic implants. After months of extensive research Fenlow was able to create a more advanced version of the implants. He promised to deliver dozens of Reploids armed with the implants to help the Brelac achieve a swifter victory. This was Fenlow's and Carp Technologies darkest secret. These were highly treasonous acts that would certainly earn Fenlow and others within Carp Technologies a swift death sentence.

"These Reploids in the hands of your military could pose a problem," Mariner stated.

"They're no threat. There's only three of them. The military will make limited use of their abilities," Fenlow assured Mariner. "And I've already taken steps to diminish their effectiveness. But they're not important. Carp's board of directors have decided to move forward with Operation Broad Axe. I have to do what I can to insure that the plan is successful. This means that I have to begin some of the more advanced projects that I've been working on."

"And you need my help to pull all this off," Mariner added. His toothy face turned silent as he studied Fenlow. "Let him go," he growled to the guards escorting Fenlow. Both guards raised their left hands to their heads in a military salute and exited the ballroom with haste.

"Fix this man a seat next to mine," Mariner blared out. "He's my guest of honor."

The attendants serving food and drink quickly provided a place at the table on Mariner's right side. As soon as Fenlow sat down next to Mariner he found a dinner plate waiting for him. It was loaded with enough food to feed three people. Fenlow could tell by this banquet that the war was certainly not hurting the Brelac. They had plenty, obviously took what they wanted and ruthlessly fought to hold onto it. Fenlow began to eat heartily, feeling confident that he had made the right decision in coming here. Working with the Brelac would certainly suit his needs.

Fenlow thought that this was the perfect time to get a little more background on his allies. "If you don't mind my asking, there's something that I need to know. Old Earth. What happened after the great exodus?"

Mariner laughed. "The great exodus. I vividly remember the details. A few thousand of Earth's fittest soaring off to find a new home among the stars. At the same time leaving a few thousand sick bastards to die. Only they didn't all die. They kept working to find a cure for pandora's simplex. Then one day a serum was developed. It proved to be effective, but not without a cost. It's long term side effect was to render it's subjects sterile."

"Sterility or the virus," said Fenlow. "Extinction either way. That explains the fact that you Brelac are Reploids yourselves."

"I'm not surprised that you found that out. But yes. After the virus was conquered there was no new births reported for several years. It was feared that the Human race would still die out. Then geneticists developed an in-vitro process of cloning Human subjects. Replication centers were built in every major city. Every citizen was required by law to donate cells for reproduction. The in-vitro process was slow. It took months for the clones to mature inside their life support tanks. Then the birth of the first cloned in-vitro children brought a new problem. The pandora simplex had introduced defective genes into many of it's victims. The children were born with leathery skin and thick scabs. Geneticists were unable to remove the defects. Over the years the cloning process advanced to a point where we could produce fully grown adults. Fully educated by a wealth of data downloaded from microchips implanted within their brains. But the mutations also advanced. Now we Humans of Old Earth have become what you see today."

Fenlow nodded. "Survivors. Strong enough to conquer pandora simplex and the United Protectorate."

Mariner's story had confirmed Fenlow's theory about the Brelac. That they were cloned descendants of those who had not joined the mass exodus from Old Earth. They had gradually evolved into the Brelac. A mutation caused by a virus that nearly wiped out Humanity centuries ago. Fenlow looked around at the scaley, lizard-like faces that surrounded him and wondered if Humanity on Old Earth had truly survived.

CHAPTER 6

▼

Colin awoke with a splitting headache. That was understandable, he thought to himself. Considering that he had survived the crash when the Brelac had shot down the ship that he and the others were traveling in. Colin now learned that the chaos was far from over. He found himself hanging upside down from the ceiling of a cavernous room. A short distance from the floor. He was hanging next to Diane, who was still unconscious.

The room itself was an enormous warehouse. Colin saw groups of shiny metallic and dark plastic containers stacked on top of each other. Large and small. Square and cylindrical. At the far end of the warehouse Colin also saw rows of tables that were holding military hardware. Colin theorized that the owner of this warehouse was trying to collect as many arms as he could. He identified weapons of all shapes and sizes. Rifles, pistols, swords, grenades and hand held missiles. At the far end of the warehouse Colin also noticed a short flight of metal steps leading up to a huge metal door. This possibly lead to the outside.

Colin tried to move his arms but discovered that they were tightly bound at the wrists by a thick leathery strap. A much longer strap bound his legs at the ankles. Diane was bound in the same manner. The length of the straps went up through two metal hooks affixed to the ceiling, then lead down to the concrete floor where they were firmly tied to another hook. Near the hook were several cardboard boxes filled with scrap metal and rusting tools. It was there that Colin caught sight of he and Diane's captors.

There were two scowling individuals. One was a muscular man wearing a pair of shorts and a hooded cape both made from scaley reptile skins. He was accompanied by a seven foot tall giant with a massive build. He was dressed in black tight fitting coveralls and thick black boots studded with metal spikes. The left side of his face was hidden by a black leather mask, also studded with spikes. The unexposed right side of his face was heavily scarred by large ashen callouses.

Colin felt that there was something familiar about these two. He searched his memory to find the answer but his mind was clouded. It was like trying to locate a coin that was dropped into a pool of murky water. Then it suddenly dawned on him that these two could both be Hellborn. The Hellborn were the children of criminals who had escaped from prison colonies on various planets and lived in the wild. Small bands of Hellborn were known to attack lone travelers who foolishly ventured into their territories. They were savage fighters but many of them were poorly organized and used crude weapons. They often ran in the face of a more powerful force.

Colin heard Diane give out a moan. She began to stir and regained consciousness.

"Where the hell are we?" she demanded.

Diane was as confused by their surroundings as Colin was. The last thing that they expected was to wake up hanging upside down from the ceiling of a warehouse. Now the question that came to Colin's mind was what would happen to them next?

The huge Helborn finally addressed them. "Glad to see that you're finally awake," his crisp baritone voice boomed out.

Colin considered the Hellborn's greeting to be friendly enough. "Is it possible for you to let us down from here?"

Colin gained a response from the Hellborn. Unfortunately it was a negative answer to his request. "I went through all the trouble of hanging you up there for a reason. It makes it easier for me if I have to kill you."

Colin did not like the sound of that.

Diane decided to try her hand at negotiating with the Hellborn. "Look, you'd better do yourself a big favor and cut us down from here right now. You'll avoid a hell of lot of trouble. We're both very important members of the Protectorate military. And they're bound to come looking for us."

"Threats from citizens don't impress me," the Hellborn snorted with contempt. "Especially threats from the military."

Colin caught onto the word, citizens. A derogatory term that Hellborn used to refer to anyone within the protectorate who were more civilized than themselves. The Hellborn considered themselves to be outlaws within the Protectorate and frowned at the notion of integrating back into so-called normal society. They were feral sociopaths who considered weaker beings as deserving prey.

"There wasn't much salvage on your ship," the Hellborn continued. "Since you ladies are such important members of the high and mighty military then I think I'll see how much they're willing to pay to get your asses back."

Colin was indignant to the Hellborn's intention. "You're holding us for ransom? Our superiors will never go for that."

"Damn right they won't," Diane snarled. "Listen up. I'm Captain Diane Christy. I'm a fighter pilot. The military is gonna want me back at any cost. And they'll most likely use force to do it. Now unless you want to find yourself buried under all this junk I advice you to cut us down now."

The Hellborn and his smaller companion both laughed at Diane's bluster. He stepped menacingly closer to her. "Well, Captain Diane Christy. I'm Vic De Boer. I may be just a lowly merchant but my boys and I control this region. And I've got enough firepower stored here to hold off an army. But just keep in mind that if your pals want to pick a fire fight then you'll both be the first ones to die."

Colin suddenly realized that his and Diane's survival were not the only ones that were in jeopardy. "What about our friends? Are they still alive?"

"Don't worry about them. They're already sold," Vic told Colin.

Colin detected an ominous tone to that reply. "Sold?"

Vic did not answer. He turned away from his prisoners and issued orders to his Hellborn minion. "I've got some business to take care of. Finish cataloging the instruments that we pulled from their ship. Then get started on the scrap metal dumpsters. They're both full so you'll have to wheel them out and empty them."

Vic took a final look back at his two prisoners. "Take the girl to help you. She should be easy enough to manage. Just don't be all day. We've got a lot of other things to do."

Vic walked away. His hulking body disappeared behind a tall stack of boxes.

The Hellborn pulled out a long dagger from a pocket in his shorts. He went over to the prisoner's straps. With a single stroke his blade sliced through one of the straps. Diane screamed when she suddenly dropped to the floor. Her arms hit the floor first. Then she painfully slammed onto her back. The Hellborn reached down and cut the straps from around Diane's ankles and wrist. Diane rose cautiously. Unsure of what would happen next.

The Hellborn slid his dagger back into his pocket. He scanned Diane from head to foot, then gave an approving nod. "Scrap metal dumpsters is a big job. We got a lotta work ahead of us."

Diane was quickly insulted by what this ragged vagrant was suggesting. "Pal, I'm a fighter pilot. I aint' no laborer. And I don't plan on staying here so why don't you cut my friend down and show us the way out?"

The Hellborn acted quickly to punish Diane for her insolence. He grabbed her by her hair and lifted her up off the floor. Colin was surprised at how easily the Hellborn was able to wield Diane. His strength matched the indomitable appearance of his thickly muscled arms. Listening to Diane's agonized yelps Colin could imagine the pain that she was going through. Feeling as if her entire scalp were being ripped from her head.

"Let her go," Colin instantly protested, but not expecting the Hellborn to comply.

The Hellborn addressed Diane more forcefully. The tone of his voice grew higher. "You're gonna have to learn to show a little respect and remember who's in charge. Vic's my boss. I'm yours. When he barks you jump first. Now if you want to stay in one piece then you'll behave yourself. You do want to behave yourself, don't you?"

Diane was helpless in this position and against the Hellborn's power she had no choice but to cry out in pain and eventually yield.

"I knew you'd see things my way," The Hellborn gleefully said. He released his hold on Diane's hair and let her drop to the floor. "You be a good girl and maybe I won't have to chain you."

Diane rubbed her scalp to soothe the pain while the Hellborn looked down at her. He had a smug look on his face that Colin wanted to bash away with a heavy rock. Even though Colin barely knew Diane he felt compelled to speak out in her defense."If you hurt her then consider yourself a marked man. There won't be a planet within the Protectorate that you'll be able to hide on."

The Hellborn was not intimidated by Colin's threat. He simply charged up to Colin and delivered a solid fist into his chest. Colin coughed to regain his breath while his chest burned in agony. He gazed back at the Hellborn with a steely coldness in his eyes. It was back by a single purpose, this Hellborn's destruction. Unfortunately that goal would be difficult to achieve while being firmly bound and hanging upside down as a helpless target. Colin was frustrated by this situation. It was a most distasteful feeling.

The Hellborn turned back to Diane, who had just returned to her feet. She launched a powerful kick to the Hellborn's groin. The Hellborn was caught completely off guard by this attack. He let out a howl that reverberated throughout the warehouse. He collapsed to the floor, clutching his aching groin and curled up into a near fetal position.

Diane grinned triumphantly while repeatedly kicking the Hellborn in his back. "Pull my hair will ya!" she shouted down at him.

After witnessing Diane's reprisal Colin urged her not to waste any more time with the Hellborn. "Quick, get me down before he recovers."

Colin hoped that the Hellborn would remain whimpering on the floor for another ten minutes or so. Clearly enough time for Diane to lower him and untie him. Diane tried to loosen Colin's strap from the hook. It was tied into an intricate knot that was too tight for her to pry apart by hand.

Diane looked up at Colin. "This damn knot won't come loose. I'm gonna find something to cut it off."

"Anytime today would be fine," Colin advised.

Diane reached into one of the boxes on the floor. She picked up a large pipe wrench, two feet long.

"Are you going to beat in into submission?" Colin impatiently asked. "Get something to cut the strap. Something sharp. Something soon."

Diane threw the wrench away. She made a frantic search through the box of rusty tools and found another large pipe wrench.

An angry snarl came from behind Diane. She turned and saw the Hellborn slowly rising to his feet. A look of rage was radiating from his face. His teeth were tightly clenched. Colin had miscalculated the amount of time that it would take for the Hellborn to recover. Now he and Diane had definitely gotten on this man's bad side.

"You are gonna die real slow and painful!" the Hellborn growled through his still gnashing teeth.

"What the hell's going on?" Vic's blaring voice shouted out. He darted from behind a stack of crates and came charging to investigate the commotion.

"Run!" Colin ordered Diane. This game of cat and mouse would now become more complicated with the appearance of a second cat.

Diane turned and fled from the area.

"You couldn't handle one girl?" Vic screamed at his henchman. "Get her you idiot!"

Diane managed to get twenty feet away before a third Hellborn leaped out from behind a stack of cardboard boxes to bar her way. An obese six foot man wearing a dark hooded robe that was badly tattered.

Diane was forced to turn back to the area where Colin was hanging. Then she saw Vic and the second Hellborn charging towards her. She spied a pile of rusted garden tools laying on the floor. Among them was an ax with a badly splintered wooden handle. She quickly grabbed this weapon. It's blade fell off when she lifted it.

The second Hellborn stopped in his tracks when he saw Diane holding the ax handle. He went into a nearby crate and picked up an ax. "What the hell do you think you're going to do with that?" he impatiently asked her.

"I'm gonna bash your head open and watch your brains spill out," was Diane's morbid reply.

Vic was eager to draw this chase to a swift conclusion. "Don't play with her, idiot! Get her! Both of you!"

The Hellborn bolted towards Diane and swung his ax. Diane's reflexes were working on a hair trigger. She ducked down and missed having her head sliced off by mere inches. The ax smashed into a stack of boxes, ripping a large hole into one of them. The stack toppled and came crashing to the floor. The sound of shattering glass echoed throughout the warehouse.

"Watch the stuff you moron!" Vic cried. He pointed a finger at the obese Hellborn. "Get over there! Get her!"

The ax wielding Hellborn swung at Diane again. She jumped to the floor and cheated him a second time. The obese Hellborn pulled out a laser pistol that was hidden within his robe. He approached Diane and took aim. Diane scrambled to her feet and darted away. The Hellborn managed to squeeze off one shot that barely missed Diane and struck the floor. The ax wielding Hellborn closely dogged Diane's back. The obese Hellborn quickly joined the chase. The laser pistol in his hand made him the greater threat. Diane dove behind a wall of stacked boxes to avoid becoming a clear target. Now both Hellborn were closing in on her to put an end to this chase.

Colin struggled desperately to get free of his straps. He had to get out of this predicament and help Diane. Unfortunately that seemed to be a wish too large to fulfill. He was fearful that Vic and his henchmen would issue him a slow and violent death after they dealt with Diane. Colin cursed his helplessness. He despised the thought of just having to hang here and wait to die. As long as he was still living Colin refused to give up without a fight.

Colin looked over to follow Diane's progress. She had ran behind a wall of boxes. The obese Hellborn took several wild shots to try to either hit Diane or flush her out into the open. Diane intended to head for another wall of boxes behind her. It was then that she was met by a fourth Hellborn. A muscular, bare chested man wearing a ragged pair of blue shorts. He launched a swift blow to Diane's face. She dropped the ax handle that she was holding and fell to her back.

The Hellborn grabbed Diane by her neck in a tight grip and lifted her up from the floor. Then he hurled her through the air. Diane landed on a metal table filled with plastic and glass water containers. The impact from Diane's body caused the containers to explode, sending a huge spray of water into the air. The table collapsed. Diane did not move. If she was stunned then Colin hoped that she would get back to her feet very quickly. Her enemies were giving her no respite. Now Vic approached Diane. He picked her up as though she were a limp rag and wrapped her body in his ponderous arm. Diane regained her senses and found herself caught in Vic's painful embrace. He was slowly constricting his arm to crush her. Diane struggled wildly but Vic's power was unyielding. There was no escape.

"I was gonna keep you around. Now I see that you'd be too much trouble," Vic told Diane.

Colin began to squirm and use greater force against the strap. He strained to wiggle free of his bonds so hard that he could feel his skin being torn by them. Colin was not going to let a few small wounds stop him. He continued to struggle and added a greater intensity. He now doubt that he could do anything to help Diane. His own life depended on him getting free. He poured every bit of strength that he could summon into the task of struggling out of these straps. After a minute of this Colin could feel his head pounding with an intolerable pain, but he continued his efforts to break free.

Colin suddenly felt a strange tingling sensation filling his entire being. It overwhelmed both his mind and body. Then a blinding blue flash and a hail of sparks exploded about him. The next thing Colin knew his hands and feet were free and he felt the painful impact of his body slamming onto the hard concrete floor.

Colin felt an intense pain on his wrists. Smoking fragments of the strap were burning his skin. He quickly tore them off and was surprised when sparks flew out of his hands. What the hell is this? He asked himself. It suddenly occurred to him that this might be a manifestation of that power that he was supposed to possess. Evidently this power had generated a surge of energy that burned through the straps. Colin wondered why this power had activated itself now. Perhaps it was the stress of his efforts to break free of the straps. Whatever the reason, all Colin knew was that it could not have come at a better time.

Vic and his Hellborn thugs were dumbfounded at the sight of Colin's spectacular escape. Diane was still making a weak attempt to break free of Vic's hold.

Colin rose to his feet. "Back off and let the lady go. Or I might have to get rough," his stern warning.

The only response that Colin received were confused stares from the four Hellborn.

"I think it's time to show you just how much trouble you're getting into," said Colin with a confident swagger.

Colin raised his hands towards the obese and muscular Hellborn's. He intended to release enough energy that could instantly transform them both into charred bones. Only a few sparks jumped from Colin's fingers. This paltry effect fell short of the deadly power that he had summoned seconds ago. Colin found this blunder to be most embarrassing.

Colin's rescue attempt had gone sour. Now without his power he decided that it would be best to use a different approach to dealing with Vic. He smiled to hide his embarrassment, if not to conciliate his antagonists. "Nice place you have here, sir. I bet you do a lot of business. Do you give out free catalogs?"

The obese Hellborn aimed his weapon at Colin. Colin dropped to the floor just as the Hellborn opened fire. He swiftly crawled behind a crate for cover. Maybe I shouldn't have mentioned the word free, he though to himself. He peered around the crate and saw the ax wielding Hellborn charging towards him. He had to escape before he wound up having his head chopped off, stuffed into a jar, and thrown into a pile of other items marked half off.

The Hellborn leaped on top of Colin. Colin was an easy opponent for him to wrestle. He lifted Colin up by his neck and tossed him into the air. Colin crashed into a stack of boxes which collapsed on top of him. he was buried under dusty electronic components.

Dazed and sore Colin barely had a chance to stand. The muscular Hellborn was upon him in an instant. He roughly lifted Colin to his feet. As Colin's head cleared he found himself being shoved to the ground at Vic's feet. The ominous form of the huge man towered over him. Vic still held Diane helplessly within his embrace. Vic's eyes blazed with malicious rage. Fear began to rum rampant through Colin's mind but he was determined not to let it show. His fear would only make the situation far worse.

Colin rose and confronted Vic. "The military won't be too happy if any harm comes to us," he warned in vain.

Vic was still unimpressed by any threats from the military. A low growl emerged from deep within his throat. He began to move forward, forcing Colin back towards the other Hellborn.

Vic spat out a command in his deep toned, booming voice. "Throw him in the pit with the rejects!"

In the pit with the rejects? Colin did not know whether that meant life or death. He was not looking forward to finding out on Vic's terms

The obese Hellborn grabbed Colin's arm to drag him away. A blue flash and a burst of sparks erupted upon contact. The brute quickly recoiled when he received the jolt. Colin's power had returned.

The muscular Hellborn dove on top of Colin and forced him to the floor. He made an attempt to strangle Colin. Unfortunately for him Colin's method of defense was highly lethal. A powerful surge of energy sent coursing through the Hellborn's body blew the skin off of his back. Colin pushed the man's smoking body aside and saw that the Hellborn with the ax was moving in for an attack.

Colin swiftly rolled out of the way and the ax smashed down on the dead Hellborn's chest instead. The moist thud of the blade cleaving through flesh and bone caught Colin's ears. He was about to stand when the Hellborn pulled the blade out and took another swing at him. Colin would have surely lost his head if he had not ducked. He knew that he could not evade every attack from this savage. Plus the obese Hellborn was advancing towards him.

Colin stumbled back against a pile of debris on the floor. A quick glance revealed that he had tripped over a pile of dirt encrusted gardening tools. The shovel with it's sharp looking blade would be an adequate weapon. He snatched it up and prepared to use it to fend off the Hellborn's next attack.

The Hellborn swung the ax down at Colin's head. Colin was barely able to thrust his shovel up to parry the attack. He was keeping alert for an opportunity to use his power against the Hellborn. His hands were tingling with arcane energy. If he could manage to touch the man then his threat would be instantly removed. The obese Hellborn had his gun trained in Colin's direction but could not get a clear shot with his comrade in the way. He continued to swing his ax at Colin only to have the blade deflected by Colin's shovel.

Vic's attention was focused on the battle between his henchmen and Colin. But he still had Diane held securely in his embrace. Diane intensified her efforts to rip herself free from Vic's crushing hug. She screamed with all the force that her lungs could supply. Diane screamed again. This time the sound of anguish in her voice was replaced by a growl of brutal rage. Now she pried Vic's arm open with an ease that completely shocked him.

Still holding onto Vic's arm Diane used it to lift Vic off of his feet. She swung him around and sent his flying several feet across the warehouse and into a brick wall. Vic crashed face first into the wall with a loud thud. The impact put dozens of cracks across the wall's surface. Vic fell to the floor and lay perfectly still. A pool of blood began to expand under his head.

Both Hellborn halted their offense against Colin when they saw their boss being so easily defeated by a female. Colin's ax wielding opponent turned his back to him. Bad move, Colin thought. This was the perfect opening that he was waiting for. Instead of using his mysterious power Colin brought his shovel down on the back of the Hellborn's head. Colin was sickened by the moist sound of metal striking the man's scalp. The Hellborn instantly dropped to the floor, exposing the bloody gash on the back of his head.

Colin saw the obese Hellborn turning to aim his pistol at Diane. "Look out!" he cried to warn her. Diane jumped down behind a table holding cardboard boxes. Colin had saved Diane from being gunned down but now placed himself in the same danger. He doved down behind a dark metal crate when he saw the Hellborn whirl about. His weapon spat out a volley of laser bolts that freely bored through the crate. They came dangerously close to passing through Colin as well.

The Hellborn turned to see Diane taking cover behind a large wall of metal and plastic boxes. He opened fire and shot everything in that area. Continually shooting he would eventually hit Diane. While the Hellborn's back was turned Colin saw this chance to make a counterattack. The tingling feeling within his hands increased. An indication that the power was still present.

Colin was still vague as to how to properly use this power, but more than willing to experiment while under fire. He sprang up from behind the crate and thrust his right hand out. He visualized himself releasing the power to strike the Hellborn down. Colin was surprised when a bolt of energy discharged from his hand and to his unsuspecting enemy. Sparks leaped from the Hellborn's body. He staggered forward, then turned to face Colin.

Diane emerged from behind the wall of boxes. She rushed over to a nearby table that held a collection of weapons and snatched up a laser pistol. She quickly took aim and squeezed off four shots into the Hellborn's back. Colin discharged another energy bolt at the huge man. The Hellborn was bathed in a bright blue flash and a hail of sparks. He may have been an exceptionally strong individual but his endurance had reached it's limit under this punishment. He clumsily spun around and fell dead to the floor.

Diane ran over to Colin. She was smiling from ear to ear. "We did it. We won," she exclaimed with excitement.

"So we did," replied Colin. He was still shivering. Still tense as he looked about. He was waiting for another enemy to pop up unexpectedly. He looked over at Vic's unmoving body. Diane's display of strength was an amazing sight. "How the hell did you do that?"

"Never mind me. How the hell did you do that? Firing the lightening bolts?" Diane countered.

Colin revealed the experience of how his power came to life. "When I was trying to break free of those straps I felt this weird sensation. Then somehow I generated this energy surge that burned off the straps. You may be right about calling then lightning bolts. I think that this power is electrical in nature."

"Your experience sounds similar to what I went through," Diane explained. "Vic was crushing me. All I felt was pain. I was trying to break free. My life depended on it. Then all of a sudden I felt like something exploded inside me. I felt like I had all this energy and nothing to do with it. That's when I had the strength to pull his arm away."

"Then it seems that Blair was right about these abilities of ours," said Colin. "We couldn't have dealt with these clowns without them. Speaking of which, Blair is here someplace. We have to find him. And the others as well."

But where to look? Colin wondered. This warehouse was a huge place. A thorough search could take some time. And Colin imagined more members of Vic's gang arriving at any moment to continue the battle. It was urgent that they find the others as quickly as possible and then leave this place. Then he would have to wrestle with the problem of where they were and how they would possibly have to fight their way out of an entire city populated by raging Hellborn of every size and gender.

The Hellborn who carried he ax began to moan. The back of his head was bleeding profusely but he was still alive and regaining consciousness. Diane displayed no compassion for the injured man. She grabbed him by the back of his neck and lifted him up over her head.

"We need him alive," Colin told Diane. "He can lead us right to where the others are being held."

Diane reluctantly complied. She allowed the Hellborn to drop roughly to his knees on the hard floor but kept a firm grip on his neck.

"Where are the other members of our group?" Colin demanded.

The Hellborn's reply was an animalistic grunt as he rubbed the bleeding wound on the back of his head. Diane yanked him to his feet.

"Let's try that again in english," Diane menacingly told him.

"Over there," the Hellborn wailed, pointing towards an area to the right.

Diane released her hold on the man and shoved him in that direction. She and Colin followed him closely. They were ready to attack if he should make a threatening move or try to escape. He brought them to a wide metal plate mounted onto the floor. There were a few small slits cut into the plate. It was secured by a large rusty lock fastened to a metal hasp that was firmly attached to the floor.

"Open it," Colin instructed Diane.

Diane shoved the Hellborn aside and kneeled down to grab ahold of the plate. The metal bent like clay under the power of her hands. Ripping out the plate and throwing it across the warehouse was just as easy.

And there they were. Held prisoner in a deep square pit under squalid conditions were four dirty and ragged troopers. These individuals were strangers to Colin. No sign of Blair, Doctor Trevor or Kelly. Colin wondered how long these men were held here. From what he could see they had not bathed in quite a while. They were probably not fed regularly either. This was not only a jail but a garbage pit, Colin thought. It had a strong and pungent odor. The troopers were laying among heaps of animal bones, soiled rags, scrap paper and rusted metal debris.

The four men rose sluggishly as if to greet their captors.

"Don't be alarmed. We're here to help you," Colin told them.

Diane pulled the troopers up from the pit one by one while Colin continued to talk to them. "I'm Sergeant Colin McKenzie. This is Captain Diane Christy. We're looking for our friends. A young man, Blair Van Doren. Doctor Arnold Trevor, an older man. And a young one. Kelly Kirby."

One of the troopers was a tall and slim figured individual whose left eye was swollen shut from an obvious beating acknowledged, "Don't worry about your friends. If you're here to rescue them then it's too late. Too late for all of them."

CHAPTER 7

▼

Colin knew that he would regret jumping into this dark metal chute. As he plummeted feet first his boots and hands failed to miss every protruding bump and strip of metal. Dusty sheets of cobwebs collided with his face and clung to his skin. Diane's screams rang out from above him. She had dove into the chute right behind him. This might be a drastic method of reaching the chamber below but there was little time to spare. Kelly's life depended of how quickly they moved. At least, that's what they were told by one of the troopers that they had liberated up above. It was Diane's idea for them to jump down into this chute and stage a dramatic rescue. Colin could still hear her words of encouragement. Doesn't look so deep to me, she said. We can do this easily, she said.

Colin's long, bumpy ride had come to an end as he emerged from the chute and landed on top of a large pile of trash. Diane came close to landing on top of him. He felt the acute pain of her legs slamming onto his back. Colin was thankful that this pile of refuse was soft enough to break their fall. He and Diane might have suffered serious injuries if they had hit the hard ground from such a great height. He tried to stand but his legs would not move. A brief struggle generated a painful spasm through his legs. Colin quickly discovered that his legs were entangled within a large mass of barbed wire. He credited the wire for helping to break his fall. Even though the end result was to lock him within a tight embrace.

Colin examined his surroundings. This pile of trash that he was laying on had an unbearably rancid smell. Kelly Kirby was laying next to him. Kelly's hands were tightly bound behind his back by a dark adhesive tape. There was also a strip of tape stuck across his mouth to keep him quiet. In spite of his bondage Kelly frantically squirmed about. His muffled cries fought to burst through the tape that sealed his mouth.

Colin noticed that there were enough lights mounted on the walls for his surroundings beyond the trash heap. They were inside a huge chamber that these Hellborn used to dispose of items that they had no further use for. In the distance He saw that the trash heap was surrounded by large groups of tall cacti. Their green spiny trunks pulsated as though they were breathing. Colin could also see that the cacti were moving towards the trash heap. Pulling themselves along by the mass of thick roots and long snaking tendrils at their base.

Colin reached over and tried to tear the barbed wire free from his legs. He looked over at one group of cacti. They were getting dangerously closer. Many of their probing tendrils gave them a reach that extended almost twenty feet away. More than enough for one of the plants to reach it's intended victim and drag him closer to it's trunk. An opening formed at the top of many of the cacti's trunks. They were hungry jaws displaying rows of gleaming white fangs. Their trunks bent forward, writhing like snakes. Their jaws repeatedly snapping in anticipation of their latest meal. Colin desperately tried to pull away the barbed wire and free his legs. It was a painful endeavor. The wire was sticking to his legs as tight as his own skin. The sharp barbs jabed his hands with each grip. Colin fought harder when he thought that something touched his foot. It could have been a tendril from a cactus, or a rat scurrying past. This was not his idea of a soldier's honorable death. He imagined himself dying in battle, taking several Brelac enemies with him as he passed. The idea of being eaten by plants in a trash pit was too ignoble for him to bear.

Kelly was also frantic to get out of here. Streams of perspiration ran across his face as he struggled. Diane was still laying in an unconscious state across his chest.

"Captain Christy! Wake up!" Colin shouted. At this time he could certainly use her extraordinary strength to help him remove this accursed barbed wire from around his legs.

Unfortunately Colin would receive no immediate help from Diane. Laying on top of Kelly her body remained still and silent.

As Kelly continued to violently squirm against his bonds small puffs of flame suddenly shot out from his face. Colin lurched back when he saw streams of glowing red energy flowing out from Kelly's head. Whatever this energy was it was hot enough to ignite the soiled waste of this trash heap. Dozens of small fires were burning all around Kelly, Diane and Colin. Small fires that would grow into a large inferno. Kelly let out a muffled cry through the tape on his mouth. This situation had now gotten worse. Now it would seem that they would all burn to death before the cacti reached them.

Diane started to move. She slowly sat up on Kelly's chest.

"Oh man. My back," Diane groaned.

"You think you have problems?" Colin told her. His hands still fought to unravel the barbed wire from his legs.

Kelly let out a muffled cry to get Diane's attention. The first thing that Diane noticed were the flames licking at her feet. She began to kick at the fire, only to see others surrounding her. Then she saw Kelly laying under her. She carefully removed the strip of tape from his mouth.

"Get off me!" Kelly roared at her.

Diane jumped up. "Sorry kid."

"Untie me! Hurry!" Kelly ordered.

"I could use a little help too," said Colin.

Diane easily ripped the tape from around Kelly's wrists. He screamed when he felt the tape's adhesive being pulled from his skin.

"Watch the fire," Kelly warned.

Diane leaped over to stamp out a fire that was growing closer to Colin.

"Watch the cactuses," Kelly warned.

"Some help here?" Colin impatiently reminded Diane.

Diane looked about at the horde of plants that surrounded them. Their tendrils continued to thrash about in hopes of grasping any victim with their reach. Diane began to search through the trash until she found the laser pistol that she carried. She had dropped the weapon during the fall.

"Give me a hand here," Kelly demanded. He was having difficulty trying to pull the tape from his ankles.

Diane growled, "Give me a break, kid. I still haven't dealt with the fire yet."

"Don't call me kid!" Kelly snapped at her.

Diane ignored Kelly's protest and immediately put the pistol to use. She pumped several laser bolts into a cactus, blowing it's trunk apart. She took aim and destroyed a second and third cactus. Kelly was still ripping at the tape around his ankles when two tendrils wrapped themselves around his legs. He called out to Diane. She spun around and severed the tendrils with laserfire.

Diane stamped out fires to her left and right. She spun back to her left and shot at two cacti who's tendrils were reaching her feet. She put out a fire near Kelly. He was still having trouble removing the tape.

"What a weakling," Diane grumbled. She kneeled down and easily ripped the tape with her fingers.

Diane reached down to Colin's legs. Instead of trying to unravel the tangle of barbed wire Diane carefully ripped it asunder.

Two tendrils wrapped themselves around Colin's neck and pulled. He was being dragged on his back through the trash to a hungry cactus that was waiting to meet him. Kelly was about to grab hold of Colin's ankles and try to pull him back. He was frightened by the sudden burst of sparks that leapt out from Colin's body. A charge of electricity surged through the tendrils and into the cactus. The enormous voltage caused the cactus to explode on contact.

Colin unwrapped the tendrils from around his neck just as others were reaching for him. He jumped to his feet and raised his hands to deliver his unique sting to these vicious plants. The flash of twin electrical bolts springing from his hands surprised and nearly blinded Kelly. Dozens of cacti exploded when the energy touched them. Colin shot two more bolts at a thick wall of cacti. The entire group was instantly decimated. Colin spun around and swept the area, front and back. He exploded more cacti than he could hope to count.

Diane was not going to allow Colin to take full credit for destroying these plants. Her laser pistol was still blazing away at any cactus within her sights. Burning chunks of cacti littered the area. A minute earlier Colin was afraid that he would not escape this chamber alive. Now fighting along side Diane for their collective survival he was certain that they could find some way out of this predicament.

Colin fired two bolts at another group of cacti and exploded them all. With the plants removed the trio could see a trooper waving to them in the distance.

"There's a way out of here," Colin shouted. He ran to lead the way.

The trooper was standing near a thick metal door. The moment the plants detected his presence many of them began to swarm towards him. Colin and Diane could not allow the cacti to bar their way. Laser bolts and electrical energy quickly mowed the plants down. In spite of this the cacti's ranks did not seem to diminish. In the distance there were many more left standing.

The trooper pulled the door open when the trio neared. They needed no urging to rush through the doorway and up a flight of concrete steps. The trooper swiftly pulled the door shut behind him. There was a thick metal bolt mounted on the door. He slid the bolt into a large hasp mounted on the wall. The door was securely locked. Now the remaining cacti in the chamber were left behind with only the fragments of their own dead to devour.

Colin, Diane and Kelly returned to the warehouse above. Colin was grateful for the trooper's help. "Thank you. Thank you for showing us the way out of there."

"We could have told you that there was an easier way down but you didn't wait," the trooper explained. "And we needed time to find the key. Vic likes to keep the door locked so that the cactuses won't get up here. They're his waste disposal system. They quickly devour any organic matter. They would have appreciated some fresh meat instead of the usual bones and dried out uneaten food scraps."

Kelly shuttered at the notion of becoming a meal for a mob of plants. "Maybe this Vic should consider recycling."

"We appreciate your help," said Colin "We haven't been properly introduced. I'm Sergeant Colin McKenzie. This is Captain Diane Christy."

"Captain Diane Christy. Ace pilot. You probably heard of me," Diane proudly added.

The trooper stared back at Diane. Remaining silent.

Colin continued. "And of course this is Kelly Kirby. We're supposed to be a special unit.

Silencers Squad."

The trooper introduced himself. "I'm Sergeant Cyrus Mandell. My friends are troopers Ron Jarret, Bret Regis and John Hild. We're with Paladin Squad, third combat division."

Colin noticed that the other three troopers that Mandell named were not present. "How long were you guys here?"

"Seven or eight months. I lost track of the exact time. We were riding our cycles on patrol. The four of us separated from the rest of the squad. That's when Vic and his crew jumped us and brought us here. Vic was going to sell us to the Brelac, but then he changed his mind. He wanted to keep us around for slave labor. He probably had the same idea for some of you people. I lost all hope of being rescued."

The other three troopers approached the group. They were accompanied by Blair and Doctor Trevor, who both beamed broad smiles when they saw Colin, Diane and Kelly.

"I thought we'd never see you guys alive again," Blair exclaimed with joy. "Those thugs had us locked up in a dusty pit. These troopers let us out and told us that you both just liberated the place by yourselves. But how?"

"It can only mean that their powers are functioning," Doctor Trevor revealed. Smiling.

Blair was overjoyed. "Then this means that the project is a success. I'm sorry that we weren't here to see how you handled these maniacs."

"I can still feel the burning sensation flowing within me. It's a frightening power," Kelly told Blair. "Then this explains how I started those fires down below."

"Fires?" Blair inquired. "If you say that you started fires then my theory is that you may be projecting a form of pure psionic energy. Energy amplified to a highly destructive level. It's the same basic power that fuels all of your abilities."

"I can accept that," replied Kelly. It was a logical explanation. "Now how do I turn it off before I accidently cremate myself?"

The sound of a loud and sternly toned voice echoed throughout the warehouse. "Vic! This is Danton! Come in please!"

All eyes turned to a small black box that was sitting on top of a table. A subspace communicator.

"Vic! This is Danton! Come in already!"

"Who the hell is that?" Colin wondered.

"Danton. Sounds like Major Danton." said Mandell.

"Who is this Danton?" Colin asked.

"Clive Danton. He's a Brelac major, stationed at some place called Rantraven. He's supposed to be some kind of science officer. And as far as I can see he's also one of the biggest assfaces that I ever saw. He comes here quite often with a platoon of troops. Likes to throw his weight around with the local Hellborn in order to keep them in line. He's real pals with Vic. Danton has done a lot of business with him."

"Vic! Come in!" Danton's voice boomed. He sounded more irritable. "We'll be arriving in three minutes. Have the merchandise ready for immediate transport. Danton out."

"What was that all about?" asked a nervous Kelly.

"The hell if I know but I don't like it," Diane groused. "I'm gonna go above and see what's going on." Diane ran to the stairs.

Mandell approached Colin to explain the meaning of the message. "I already told you that it's too late for your two friends. Vic made a deal to sell them to Danton."

"He sold us?" Blair exclaimed. Appalled by this news.

"Vic often sells prisoners to the Brelac and back to our side if the price is right. He was planning to sell you and the old guy for now. Hang on to Colin and Captain Christy until he decides what to do with them later. He thought that the young one, Kelly was just another kid. Vic had no use for Kelly so he dumped him into the disposal pit."

"Nobody's going to be sold off anywhere," Colin sternly declared. "This Danton is just going to have to settle for a rain check."

Diane dashed down the stairs and excitedly reported her findings to Colin. "Two attack shuttles are about to land outside. They're probably carrying a mob of Brelac. They'll be here any second."

Colin was uncomfortable with the idea of fighting the Brelac here. He and the others would be outnumbered and cornered in a building that was poorly suited to serve as a battleground.

"Kelly, you're with me. Everybody else take cover.," Colin ordered. Mandell offered Colin another option. "There's a second way out of here. It's a tunnel in the back."

"Then let's hope that the Brelac aren't using it," Colin replied. He changed his orders for the group. "Get these bodies out of sight and follow Mandell. Kelly and I will try to hold the Brelac off."

Colin make a hurried inspection of several cardboard boxes until he found what he was looking for. He pulled out a box that contained old clothing and shoes. They were dusty and had a strong mildewy odor. Colin quickly took off his coveralls and boots. Instructing Kelly to do the same. Colin picked out their new attire from the box. Two pairs of ragged blue denim shorts and dirty white sneakers. He gave Kelly a sleeveless black shirt while he selected a blue shirt that was heavily marred by reddish stains.

While Kelly and Colin changed their clothing Diane and Blair assisted the four troopers in the job of removing the dead Hellborn from view. Getting rid of them was easy. They mearly dropped the bodies into the disposal pit and let the cacti below do the rest. Diane was afraid that the wounded Hellborn, still clutching the back of his bloodied head would create a huge problem if he remained in the warehouse. Her quick solution was to drag him over to the disposal pit and dump him in.

"Vic!" a loud voice blared out from behind the door at the top of the stairs.

For an extra touch to Kelly's camouflage Colin handed him a push broom that was laying near a table. Kelly began to casually sweep the area while awaiting the arrival of their visitors. Mandell lead the others to the rear of the warehouse. They moved around a large stack of wooden crates to reach the tunnel that he spoke of. Kelly and Colin remained behind to face a dozen heavily armed Brelac who had opened the door and were now heading down the stairs.

The first one that caught Colin's attention was the leader. He was wearing a silver armband that displayed a prominent black oak leaf. This was clearly the Major Danton that trooper Mandell had described.

"Who the hell are you?" Danton rudely demanded.

Kelly did not respond to the Brelac and kept sweeping.

Colin adopted a cheerful demeanor and extended his hand in a friendly greeting. "I'm Colin McKenzie. The kid here is Kelly Kirby. We're both new here. Vic just put us on today."

Danton walked past Colin and Kelly and began to scan the area. Kelly gave Danton a "Hi," in a weak voice but was ignored. Apparently the ploy was working. Danton and the other Brelac were mistaking their ragged and dirty clothing for that of two Hellborn.

Danton was not interested in freindly gestures. "Where's Vic?" he simply asked.

Danton's troops slowly surrounded Colin and Kelly.

"Vic? He went back to the crash site," Colin said with a smile.

Danton was confused. "The crash site? Why the hell did he do that?"

"He said that there was still some equipment that he wanted to take out of that Protectorate ship. There's no telling how long he'll be gone. Maybe you can come back later."

"I'm not leaving without those two prisoners that Vic told me about!" Danton snapped back. "Bring them out!"

Colin politely explained another story to Danton. "I'm terribly sorry but Vic took the prisoners with him. He said that he'd need some labor to help carry the equipment back. Perhaps we can interest you in something else."

Colin pointed to Kelly. Kelly nervously looked about at the cardboard boxes near his feet. He quickly reached down for the first item that he saw. A long wooden stick with a dusty rubber suction cup mounted on the end.

"How about this deadly little Hellborn weapon here?" Kelly asked.

Danton slapped the instrument out of Kelly's hand. His patience was fading rapidly. "What the hell is this? I Don't want no damn plunger! Where are Vic's other guys? Where's Brace, Harper, Scab?"

Colin could not match those names with any faces. He calmly explained, "Vic took them along. He said that he needed somebody to keep an eye on the prisoners."

This was all that Danton could tolerate. He bared his fangs in an enraged snarl and lunged at Colin. He grabbed Colin by his throat and shoved him back against a table.

Colin stared back into that eyeless reptilian face. He could not see the slightest shred of humanity or compassion. There was just rage and intolerance. Dear God, this guy is intense, Colin told himself. He wondered if all Brelac were like this. And if so did they ever lighten up at all? Did they ever laugh? Did they ever trade jokes to each other or sing the tune to their favorite songs while torturing prisoners? Did they ever go to wild drunken parties and wear lampshades on their heads to make fools of themselves? The details of a Brelac's personal life was a mystery to Colin. He would ponder the issue at a later date. Right now he was more interested in ending the life of this Brelac major who was in his face.

"You think I like wastin' my time comin' out here to listen to a bunch of crap?" Danton shouted closely to Colin's face. "Something stinks! I'm not leaving until I find out what it is!"

Colin felt that it was a pity that Brelac did not wear underwear. He could have offered Danton a vital clue to follow.

Danton shoved Colin to the floor, then walked away. "Four of you keep these morons covered. If either of them tries anything shoot them both. The rest of you search this building. Something's wrong here. I'm gonna get to the bottom of it."

As Danton ordered, two of his soldiers kept their plasma rifles aimed at Kelly's head. Two others charged over to Colin and kept their weapons trained on him as he slowly sat up. They were daring them to move. The rest of the platoon spread out and began to search through the warehouse for anything that seemed suspicious.

It was Danton who first discovered a remnant of the furious battle that took place here. He jumped back after his foot stepped into a pool of liquid. Danton dipped his fingers into the liquid. He brought his fingers to his nostrils and sniffed. There would be no mistaking what this was.

"Blood!" Danton cried out.

Colin took that as a signal to take action before the Brelac did. He raised his hands at the two soldiers standing in front of him. They were caught off guard when Colin fired twin bolts of electricity that hurled them across the warehouse. Kelly decided to follow Colin's lead and raised his hands at his twin targets to try and discharge his power. Nothing happened.

The two soldiers guarding Kelly were momentarily distracted by Colin's assault. They turned their attention back to Kelly and raised their weapons to fire. Certain that he was about to die Kelly screamed and defensively raised his hands in front of his face. The plasma rifles blazed their crimson fire just as a panel of shimmering blue energy appeared in front of Kelly. The multiple plasma bolts instantly bounced off the panel and were reflected back at the soldiers who fired them. The two surprised Brelac collapsed to the floor and died at the feet of an astonished Kelly. His power had just saved his life, but not in the way that he had expected.

Kelly stood triumphantly after slaying two Brelac soldiers without raising a single finger. Colin was amazed at this uncanny manifestation of Kelly's power. Then Kelly's face quickly transformed to am image of wide eyed fear.

"Look out!" Kelly shouted. He dove to the floor. Colin turned to see Major Danton drawing his pistol from it's holster. He threw a swift electrical bolt at Danton. Danton quickly ducked down and returned fire. Two plasma bolts zipped past Colin's head. He had no time to make a second attack against Danton. The other Brelac were converging on he and Kelly's position.

Colin grabbed Kelly's arm and lead him to the back of the warehouse. They dove down between two tables holding computer keyboards. Kelly stayed close to Colin when he crawled forward. A trio of Brelac opened fire and shredded the tables and keyboards. Colin sprang up from behind the tables and hurled two bolts that knocked all three Brelac to the floor. The element of surprise had worked to his advantage. He turned to his right and struck down another Brelac who was about to aim his rifle and shoot. Until Kelly could exercise a better control over his power he was forced to contend with keeping out of harm's way and watching Colin battle the Brelac on his own.

Danton's platoon began to advance on their target's position. Colin crouched down. "We have to get out of here now. Powers or no powers. There's just too many of them," he told Kelly.

Colin began to crawl to the rear of the basement to reach the tunnel. Kelly followed close behind. Plasma bolts were burning into every box and piece of hardware around them. The Brelac's left and right flank began to move closer. Their firepower was cutting Kelly and Colin off from moving forward. They were trapped.

Neither of them paid any attention to the stack of rusted metal crates that were just a few feet in front of them. Diane suddenly burst through the crates and gunned down four surprised Brelac with her laser pistol. Colin thought that Diane was outside where it was reasonably safe. He was glad to see her when he and Kelly needed her the most.

"Let's go!" Diane shouted to them.

Colin and Kelly ran to follow Diane. They dashed into the tunnel where the others were anxiously waiting.

The group emerged from the base of a large building. It's upper floors were gutted by past bombings. They did not have a chance to get far. A small group of armed Protectorate troopers stopped them in their tracks. They seemed to be unprepared to meet up with this odd assortment of persons.

Blair was overjoyed to see Protectorate troopers. He smiled and moved towards them with open arms. "My God. Am I ever glad to see you guys. There's a gang of Brelac inside and—"

"Freeze!" a trooper ordered Blair. He raised his rifle. "Move an inch and I'll take your head off."

Blair wanted to assure the troopers that he and the others were not a threat. "It's ok. We're on your side."

"Shut up!" the trooper snapped "Say another word and I'll burn a hole through your face. Don't any of you move. Keep your hands where I can see them. Do it now."

That belligerent attitude seemed familiar. Colin wondered it this trooper was somehow related to Diane. He joined the others as they slowly raised their hands to comply.

CHAPTER 8

▼

The Morthos star system was once a prime industrial, mining and agricultural center that provided large supplies of food and manufactured goods for the Protectorate's colony worlds. Today it's five inhabited planets are conquered by the Brelac and converted into a temporary headquarters for Brelac operations in this sector of the quadrant. The bulk of the Brelac space fleet rested here at the seven gargantuan sphere shaped star bases that were stationed at the outer rim of the system. Hundreds of the Brelac's large conical battle cruisers, their manta ray shaped attack carriers and larger battleships were docked along the outer hulls of the star bases. Fleets of ships departed the system only to be replaced by other swarms of ships that were returning from combat to receive repairs and fresh supplies. Multiple divisions of ground units were housed in the expansive military bases that were established on the planet Morthos Three.

In an underground level of Rantraven base, a major military installation, Doctor Fenlow was working in the laboratory that the Brelac had provided for him. He was examining the bio monitor on an incubation tube. He noted the temperature reading, ninety eight degrees. Fenlow was confident that there would be no complications with the organism that was growing inside. Immersed in the warm nutrient liquid the organism would soon mature. Then Fenlow would prepare for the second phase of it's development.

In dealing with the Brelac Fenlow found that they were quite generous. They gave him this huge laboratory that was loaded with an abundance of supplies. Behind him was a powerful computer sitting on a metal workbench. Several other pieces of equipment here were also highly advanced.

Fenlow had no qualms about being here. He was not haunted by the specters of the men that he killed. It did not matter if he was branded as a traitor. He and Carp Technologies were working to save the future of Human kind. Some small sacrifices would have to be made. He was working to insure that the United Protectorate survived this war and continued to flourish. Then he would be hailed as the savior of his people.

The door behind Fenlow slid open. One of his new allies entered the laboratory. Major Clive Danton. When Fenlow first met Danton he instantly labeled the major as a pompous brain dead yes man to Mariner. In Fenlow's opinion Danton was a non-intellectual animal whose only solution to any problem was to shoot it repeatedly and burn the remains. He was also Fenlow's official guardian. Or guard, as the case may be. He personally saw that Fenlow received everything he needed. He was also keeping a close eye on Fenlow. Fenlow tolerated Danton, thinking that this particular Brelac would not be around forever. And that in any given situation one has to take the good with the bad.

"Hello Major," Fenlow greeted with a cold voice. Not bothering to face Danton.

"I'm just checking up to see if there's anything you might need," he said to Fenlow. "I also have an unusual report to relay to you. I got into a fight on Voran with two strange Hellborn. They called themselves Colin McKenzie and Kelly Kirby."

Those two names instantly caught Fenlow's attention. He turned from the incubation tube and faced Danton.

Danton continued. "It seemed that these two Hellborn possessed some kind of strange abilities. One of them had the ability to shoot bolts of energy from his fingertips. The other produced an defensive energy shield that reflected our firepower. I tried to bring them both back with me for examination. Dead or alive. An unexpected attack by Protectorate troopers forced me and my men to back off. What do you make of this?"

Fenlow spat out a brief burst of laughter. He knew everything about these two Strange Hellborn, as Danton called them. The names Colin McKenzie and Kelly Kirby were the key. "The creatures that you described were not Hellborn. They're Reploids. Two of the three advanced Reploids that my government captured. They were supposed to be out in space aboard Lodestar."

"Well they're not at Lodestar. They're back on Voran," Danton countered. "Possibly planning to retaliate against you for defecting. And what if your people should somehow create more of them?"

"Impossible. We hold all the proper resources to create Reploids. Especially the advanced class. I have nothing to fear from this matter."

"Just the same, as a precaution I've asked General Lagar to place the entire system under alert and increase security."

"Sounds like you're afraid," said Fenlow.

"No. Nonsense," Danton scoffed. "Only a fool relaxes his guard in the face of an unknown threat."

Fenlow laughed. "I was right. You are afraid."

Danton was offended by that charge. "In war you keep your guard up at all times and never let your enemy off the hook. That's why we've been able to handle you Humans so well. Wouldn't you agree?"

Fenlow glared back at Danton through venomous eyes. Danton was clearly trying to provoke him into a confrontation. Fenlow was not about to waste his time on any petty arguments. He simply stared at Danton for a moment, then addressed him quietly.

"I agree that you Brelac have the upper hand in this war. That's why I'm here. To make sure that you keep it. As for the Reploids, I don't consider them to be a threat. They're obsolete when compared to my current projects. But if it will make you feel any better I'll handle them. After all, they are my creations. Take me to the base's robotics research lab. I have a plan that's guaranteed to put the Reploids out of action."

CHAPTER 9

▼

Since coming to Nocturne, A heavily fortified military base on the planet Trillion, Colin, Diane and Kelly were immediately placed in a detainment cell. Colin sat with Kelly on a metal bench and watched Diane impatiently pace back and fourth. He was just as infuriated as they were at the thought of being locked up like prisoners of war. Especially by their own side. They had not seen or heard anything from Blair for three days. With their powers Colin knew that he, Diane and Kelly could easily break free of this frail prison. But such a drastic action would only make matters worse. As much as he hated the idea they would have to remain here until the powers that be decided their fate.

At least they were not wasting most of their time sitting idle. Colin was coaching Kelly in gaining control over his power. Kelly quickly learned how to manipulate the intense psionic energy that he generates. With a point of a finger he could send a stream of fiery energy to melt holes through the metal bench with little effort. He could also summon a shield of defensive energy at will. And in any shape that he desired. Square or round. Panels of the glowing blue psionic energy that were small enough to shield his hand or large enough to cover an entire wall. Kelly was proud to know that his energy shields were quite durable, withstanding an assault against Colin's powerful electrical bursts and the titanic strength behind Diane's pounding fists.

Kelly wanted to experiment with other applications for his power. Diane was not comfortable with the idea of being confined in this cell while Kelly conducted potentially dangerous experiments with a power that he was just becoming familiar with. Colin also voiced his fears, more to ease Diane's worries. We won't be here much longer, he kept assuring them both. For now they could just sit back and relax. There would be plenty of time for Kelly to experiment with his powers when he gets out into larger spaces.

The door to the cell suddenly slid open. Then Blair, Doctor Trevor and General Larkin entered the cell. In the presence of a high ranking general Colin and Kelly jumped up from the bench and stood rigidly at attention next to Diane, who had already assumed the same position.

"Be at ease and relax," Larkin said. "You're the ones that deserve the respect after all you've been through. If it weren't for the three of you Blair and Doctor Trevor would be in the hands of the Brelac. Or perhaps dead. And you also rescued those four troopers in the process. Your actions are truly heroic."

Colin silently agreed with Larkin. He, Diane and Kelly were indeed heroes. But he thought that it would be best to appear modest. "We were just doing a soldier's duty, sir. Fighting the enemy and protecting our comrades lives."

"Duty or not, you saved us from those Hellborn. And ultimately the Brelac," Blair stated. "You guys are heroes in my book. We should go to president Drennen and recommend you all for medals. I'm sure that Doctor Fenlow would agree."

"Doctor Fenlow?" Colin inquired.

Doctor Trevor stepped forward to explain. "He's the head of the project that gave you three your powers. I'm quite sure that he would be happy to meet you and see that you are all alive and functioning properly."

"Assuming that we can find him," Larkin added. "The man vanished shortly after you left. We contacted Lodestar but they told us that they haven't seen him. No one at Carp has seem him either."

"He's probably off hiding someplace working where he can't be disturbed," Doctor Trevor theorized. "He's probably working on some special project. I wouldn't worry. In time he'll show up."

"I hope so. His insight on this project could be vital," Larkin explained. "But in the meantime we're finally letting you out of here and reassigning the three of you to other duties within the base."

Diane smiled, nodding in approval. "About time, sir. I was starting to go nuts in here. I'm ready to get back to my squadron."

Larkin hesitated before responding. "For the moment we have other plans for you, Captain."

"The three of you are an experimental unit," said Doctor Trevor. "There are still many aspects of your abilities that you haven't explored. Until we can consult with Doctor Fenlow and develop you to your full potentials I've suggested to General Larkin that we should hold off deploying you for any missions."

"It makes sense," Blair added. "You'll want the full range of your powers working when the time comes to deal with the Brelac."

"Escort them to the command center. Captain Roberts will give them their new assignments," Larkin ordered. "In the meantime I have several pressing matters to deal with. It's been a pleasure meeting you all. I'll check up on you from time to time."

Larkin left the cell and went his separate way. Colin felt apprehensive about the idea of a General making surprise visits. But not as apprehensive as he felt about his new assignment.

"I wonder what kind of new jobs they're gonna give us," Diane said. "Since we've got all these fancy powers I'm ready to see some action."

"You won't see any action for a while," said Blair. "Chances are you'll be given jobs within the base."

Diane scoffed. "Not any damn grunt work I hope. I'm a fighter pilot and an officer."

Kelly let out an irritated sigh. "We're soldiers. We go where we're told."

"You look a little young to be calling yourself a soldier, kid," Diane sarcastically chided.

"For the last time I'm not a kid!" Kelly snapped.

Colin was not in the mood to listen to Diane and Kelly argue. "I feel a lot better knowing that you two will be separated."

"And I feel a lot better knowing that the three of you are staying here. You're not ready to take on any dangerous missions."

Diane chafed under Blair's conviction "We already took on the Hellborn and the Brelac."

"We were lucky and they were taken by surprise. I don't want to gamble my life on it happening again," Colin scolded. "Maybe we can take the time to learn more about our powers. We were making progress with Kelly. There still might be things that Blair and Doctor Trevor can tell us about our own."

Blair offered information that he previously withheld. "The three of you have specially designed psionic implants within your brains. They amplify the brain's level of psychic activity. Each implant is regulated differently. I don't understand the exact nature of this regulation, but this is how each of you developed a different power. Diane's power manifested itself in the form of increased strength. Colin gained a form of increased electro-chemical activity. And we've already established that Kelly manipulates psionic energy in it's pure form. There could be several other applications for each of your abilities. We just have to be patient and train you to find them."

Diane grumbled, "And how long will that take? The Brelac aint' gonna wait for us to complete any training sessions."

"What about this Doctor Fenlow?" asked Kelly. "You said that he can help us."

"If he ever decides to show up," replied Blair. "He knows far more about the implants than we do. We could certainly use his knowledge."

"But until then you three have new jobs to go to," Doctor Trevor reminded them. "You'd better not keep Captain Roberts waiting."

Captain Roberts awaits, Colin silently mused. As Kelly stated, soldiers go where they are told. Although Colin was not happy with the idea of taking on a new assignment while there were several gaping holes exposed in his life. The memories of his past were as unclear as his future. He still felt incomplete. Colin began to resent Blair and Doctor Trevor for not doing enough to help him. Or helping Diane and Kelly. Colin's mind recalled the cheery rhyme that pertained to military life and government service. Orders are obeyed and secrets will be made. He wondered if Blair and Doctor Trevor were keeping some great secret to themselves.

Colin could not conjure any logical reason why they would withhold any vital information about his physical or mental condition. Whatever answers were waiting for Colin he would have to be patient before he could find them. For now he reminded himself that Captain Roberts was waiting. There would be new work laid out for Colin.

CHAPTER 10

▼

For two weeks life at Nocturne was uneventful for Colin. And he was also terribly bored with his new job in the quartermaster's corps. He was assigned to a small storeroom where he worked alone. Wearing his loose fitting dark blue uniform and shiny black boots Colin spent his time standing in front of this sturdy metal dutch door handing out supplies. He also took inventory and positioned buckets to catch water that regularly leaked from the ceiling. Colin put his best efforts into his job and gained great compliments from his immediate superior, Captain Roberts. But regardless of his performance Colin still felt that his efforts could be devoted towards something that was far less mundane.

Colin knew that he was not the only one who was assigned to an undesirable job. Blair occasionally stopped by to chat and give him reports about Kelly and Diane. They were also unhappy with their new functions. Diane was eager for a combat mission. As a last resort she would even settle for guard duty. Instead of getting either position she was thrown a curve and assigned to an excavation crew within the subterranean levels of the base. They were just one of several crews that worked to dig out tunnels and expand chambers.

Diane reported that her co-workers were amazed at her inhuman strength. She could move large rocks far easier and faster than any machine. She could carry heavy loads of equipment and supplies without strain. With her help her crew was days ahead of schedule. Her co-workers considered her to be invaluable. Although there were a few who felt uneasy being around a person with her strength.

Diane heard rumors circulating throughout the tunnels that she was not really a person. She heard one story about her being an advanced prototype robot that was being tested by the military. Another stated that she was some sort of mutant that was grown in a laboratory. Colin felt sympathy for the person who was starting these wild rumors. Diane was already irritated about her job. She would relish the opportunity to vent her incendiary frustrations out on a troublemaker. On the rare occasions that Diane was not in a bad mood She would relate stories to her co-workers about shooting down two hundred and thirty enemy fighters, and that she would not be stuck digging tunnels until the end of the war.

Kelly was assigned to the maintenance corps. Blair recalled the bitterness in Kelly's voice a week ago when he described how much he disliked mopping floors, emptying trash containers and cleaning latrines. Poor Kelly, Colin thought. He started out being so compliant to follow orders. Two days ago Blair described Kelly's current assignment. His crew was working to expand the base's command center by installing computer systems and communications equipment. Kelly started out as an aide to one of the older technicians. That's when he realized that he possessed an extensive technical knowledge. He was able to adeptly read electrical schematics and install instruments on his own. He even analyzed the technician's plans and offered a few improvements. That was an act that placed a strain on Kelly's relationship with his co-workers. Kelly learned that many of the seasoned technicians resented the idea of being overshadowed by an overeager newcomer. Especially if that newcomer appeared to be a know it all teenager.

While Colin, Diane and Kelly were pursuing their unappealing jobs Blair was putting his medical skills to good use. He was treating wounded troopers in the base's infirmary. Colin did not envy Blair's daily twelve hour shifts. But after listening to Blair describe his activities Colin sensed that the young man was gaining a great feeling of accomplishment by helping to save lives. Colin also began to feel jealous of Blair. His deeds in the infirmary may not have been flamboyant as those of a special forces commando, but using his life saving medical skills was still regarded as heroic. With his arcane power to generate electricity Colin imagined himself receiving many accolades as a legendary hero, performing many dangerous missions against the Brelac to bring the war to a victorious conclusion. But the cold, hard fist of reality punched holes through his frail daydreams. At the present time he was confined here in this dank storeroom handing out supplies while listening to the nonstop drips of leaking water from the ceiling filling the buckets on the floor.

Colin looked at the new digital watch that he had purchased for himself. The time was 4:56 P.M. Close enough to his 5:00 P.M. closing time. He opened the bottom half of the dutch door and exited the storeroom. Complying with regulations he closed and locked both halves of the door. The storeroom was now secure and he was free to leave for the evening.

Colin made no definite plans for later. For now he was only concentrating on the biting hunger that haunted him for hours. He stepped out of the building and into the chilly night air. Colin still had an aversion to the cold. He was thankful that he had a job indoors where he could remain comfortable and warm.

It was a short walk across the base for Colin to reach the building that served as the cafeteria. Inside he found that it was not too crowded. The line was short. Colin was glad that he had arrived after the majority of the dinner crowd had gathered. Colin got in line and picked up a tray with a knife and fork. He steadily moved along the line and reached the servers. He savored the aroma of chipped beef with gravy. The female server issued him a large helping. Colin received mashed potatoes with gravy, boiled carrots and string beans. For a beverage he selected a steaming hot cup of coffee. With his meal complete Colin moved away from the line and headed for an empty table near the wall.

While eating his dinner Colin silently studied the camaraderie that was taking place around him. At the other tables groups of troopers sat and ate together. The sounds of laughter boomed out from joyful faces. Others were engaged in less boisterous conversation. At one table he even spied a card game being played among a group of four troopers. It would appear that Colin was one of the few persons who were sitting alone. Since arriving at Nocturne Colin was used to eating alone. He had no desire to mingle with any of these people. He was too submerged in his personal thoughts to concentrate on making friends. While staring into his tray he brooded about his identity. Why his past memories were incomplete, and where his future would take him. He still had no memories of a childhood or of any relatives. Nor of any friends, save for the intrusive trooper Ed Driscol. To this day Colin could still express little love for the man.

Colin also wondered why he was experiencing the same series of dreams night after night. In one dream he was laying on the ground. His body was being soaked by the rain. There was an angry man beating him, kicking him. He was snarling and shouting a stream of obscene curses at Colin with each painful blow. Colin could not see this man's face. There was only a dark shadow standing over him like a storm cloud of hate. The assault grew more violent and painful until Colin was jolted awake. He suffered through this unexplained nightmare for the past two weeks. Never revealing the experiences to anyone.

Colin's other dream replayed his activities during the day. He recognized himself working in his storeroom, issuing supplies to troopers, sitting at his desk doing paperwork, and emptying the buckets that caught water from the leaking pipes in the ceiling. Colin had little concern for these dreams, since they did not have the same disturbing impact as the other dream. Colin did not know what this dream meant, But as with the other questions concerning his life he felt that he could depend on noone but himself to unearth the answers that he needed.

As Colin continued to eat and swim in his quagmire of thoughts he noticed a small group of men enter the cafeteria and step in line. Colin was about to disregard their presence when he noticed that there was a certain Lieutenant among the group. Colin focused on the tall white male's face. He began to recognize the man. A name quickly popped into Colin's head. Yates. Lieutenant Paul Yates.

Colin cracked a smile and fought to restrain a burst of laughter. The last thing that he expected to see here was his former commanding officer. As well as a few other men from his old squad. Colin recognized some of their faces. In the past he had never acted friendly towards these men. Now being out of the squad after all this time Colin wondered if this would be a perfect time to get reacquainted. There was also the chance that the Lieutenant or some of these other men could reveal a few vital facts about his past life.

Colin's gaze never left sight of Lieutenant Yates. The man steadily moved down the line, having servers dispense his meal onto his tray. Colin began to grow nervous while wondering when he should get up and approach these men. Should he go now or wait until they take their seats and ask to join them? Colin was startled out of his musings when a person roughly pulled out the chair at his right and plopped down. Slamming their tray onto the table. It was Captain Diane Christy. She was the last person that Colin expected, or even wanted to see at this time.

"Well, Sergeant McKenzie. What a surprise to see you here," Diane said in a jocular tone. "I haven't heard from you for nearly two weeks."

"I know," Colin's sober reply. He had little enthusiasm in talking to Diane.

"So, what have you been up to," Diane asked. She jabbed her fork into her chipped beef and loaded it into her mouth.

Colin never broke his gaze from Lieutenant Yates. "Nothing special. Just doing my job," Colin's brusque answer.

"Your job? I assume that you're still working in that leaky storeroom," Said Diane.

"What else am I going to do? I just follow orders until something better comes along," Colin told her.

Diane gave a short laugh. "I've got news for you, Sarge. You're never gonna get ahead by just sitting on your ass and waiting for someone to notice you. You've got to take what you want. Like myself. I'm a Captain. I'm not gonna keep doing this hard labor crap for the rest of the war. Yesterday I put in for a transfer to a fighter squadron. I should hear about it any time now."

"Maybe you should be packing," Colin grimly suggested, hoping that she would consider the advise and leave.

Colin still followed Lieutenant Yates as he and the other men sat at a table at the far end of the cafeteria.

Diane noticed that Colin was doggedly staring at the group. "Friends of yours?"

"That depends," said Colin. He had heard enough from Diane. He rose from his seat, deciding to act.

Colin slowly strode over to the table where the Lieutenant and the other men were seated. In his mind he held the vision of Lieutenant Yates expressing surprise over his unexpected appearance. Giving him a firm handshake and welcoming him to sit down among the others so that they could intensely grill him on his activities these past weeks. The men ate, drank and laughed to humorous tales that they exchanged to themselves. Their festive mood evaporated and the men all grew silent when they saw Colin drawing near to their table.

Colin waved his hand in greeting. "Lieutenant Yates. How have you been?" he meekly asked.

For a moment the Lieutenant quietly glared back at Colin. As he stared back into The Lieutenant's unsmiling face Colin could sense a fog of animosity radiating from the man.

"This is a dream," the Lieutenant stated. Still frowning at Colin. "No, make that a nightmare. I took a shot to the head and right now I'm in a coma having a bad dream. In that nightmare I'm seeing that murdering son of a bitch, Sergeant Colin McKenzie."

Colin was shocked and confused by the Lieutenant's stinging words. He stood silently while the Lieutenant continued with his hostile tirade.

"You're the last person that I've ever expected to see here. Here in a Protectorate military base. Just strolling along like you're one of us."

"I am," Colin dared to correct. "At least, I was, until I left your command."

"You left my command?" the Lieutenant returned. For a moment he laughed. "That's an interesting way to put it. But I think I like my version a hell of a lot better. You remember, don't you? When I nearly caved your face in back at Meridan."

"I don't understand," said Colin.

"You don't understand?" the Lieutenant snarled back. His anger mounting. "Maybe I beat you in the head a little too hard. That's the only way you could have forgotten about the two men that you killed."

"The men that I killed?"

"Yeah. Troopers Lance and Meyers. You shot Lance. And Meyers, I don't know how you did it but you burned him to a crisp. Couldn't recognize his body after you were done with him. And I'll never understand what Driscol did to trooper Craven."

Killing fellow troopers in cold blood? Colin was skeptical of the charge. Until he began to scan through his past memories when he served under the Lieutenant's command. There was that mission on Meridan, the cold and rainy planet. He remembered being in the forest. Being wet. There was a downed Brelac shuttle craft. Trooper Driscol was shadowing him, as usual. He saw several white cylinders. There was a firefight. Trooper Driscol was killed.

The weapon's fire was furious. He saw himself using his powers to fatally electrocute a Protectorate trooper. The acrid smell of burning flesh penetrated his nostrils.

As Colin Looked into the Lieutenant's enraged face he recalled the nightmares that he was having. Of laying on a wet ground during a heavy rain. The unknown person hovering above him, mercilessly beating him while spitting out an intense verbal assault. The face of that man started to become more clear. It was Lieutenant Yates who was relentlessly pummeling him in his nightmares. But now it was not just a simple bad dream. It was one of the past memories that Colin sought. A sick feeling now overwhelmed Colin. It was like a cold metal spike being rammed into the center of his stomach. The Lieutenant had tried to kill him out of retribution for the deaths of those two men.

"Oh, that," Colin meekly replied. That was the only response that his perturbed mind could summon.

"Oh, that?" the Lieutenant shouted. "You sound like you're talking about a couple of overdue books that you took from the library. I'm talking about the lives of three men. Lives that you and Driscol wiped out."

The Lieutenant's charge caused Colin's guilt to rise. He felt like crawling under a table and hiding his face. But he also felt compelled to make an effort to atone for his past actions. He was not losing sight of his purpose here. To establish a friendly dialog with the Lieutenant.

"I'm sorry," Colin stated in a soft voice.

The Lieutenant sprang up from his seat and knocked his tray off of the table with a swift backhand swipe. He stormed from around the table and approached

Colin, stopping just a few inches away from his face. The Lieutenant's voice exploded into a fiery rage. "And you think that a petty little, I'm sorry is gonna fix things? I'm sorry too. Sorry that we didn't put your ass down back on Meridan the way we did Driscol. I'm sorry that I listened to Trooper Jones, telling me that you might be a useful prisoner. So I cut you a break and turned your ass over to covert intelligence. But apparently they didn't consider you to be too valuable, or a threat. So they turned you loose. Now here you are, back in my face."

Colin began to reconsider approaching the Lieutenant. His agitation and hostility created a wall that was too thick and high for Colin to attempt to traverse. "This was a mistake. I just thought that we could have a friendly conversation and discuss old times. I don't want any trouble so I'll just leave."

Colin turned to walk away from the Lieutenant. That was when he felt a sudden sharp impact strike him on the back of his head. The force combined with the pain were enough to topple him. He helplessly watched the floor draw close to his face within a second. His forehead pounded against the hard surface, leaving him dazed for a brief moment. As he tried to rise he listened to a renewed verbal assault from the Lieutenant.

"You want to talk about old times? Lemme refresh your memory. My memory of two trusted soldiers under my command turning on the entire squad to kill their own. My memory of how stupid I felt having traitors and murderers hanging under my nose. The memory of how you shot me four times. The reaction that I got from those troopers wives and families when I told them the bad news. And now here you show up wanting to us to be old buddies?"

An unidentified trooper shouted out from the mob surrounding the Lieutenant, "Maybe we should finish the job that you started back on Meridan."

A chorus of voices within the group echoed the trooper's sentiment. Colin saw hatred in every face. He was now placed in a complicated dilemma. These men were clearly expressing a hostile intent towards him. He had to protect his survival. But would he do so by having to fight his fellow troopers? The revelation that he had previously murdered two men was consuming his mind. He did not want to be mounted with more guilt by harming any of these men, with or without his power. He was already attacked once. Would they allow him to leave in peace? Or would he be attacked again and severely injured?

Colin defensively held up his hands. "Listen guys. I'm leaving. I didn't come here to fight anybody."

"You might not leave until you do," the Lieutenant's ominous reply. Driscol's dead. Now we've got you to deal with."

The group of men were becoming more agitated. One of them roughly shoved the table aside and they all approached Colin. People sitting at nearby tables were quick to abandon their trays and scurry away from the area. Colin did not expect to receive help from anyone here. They would be content with standing and watching the carnage while preserving their own personal safety.

"I still owe you for trying to kill me," said the Lieutenant. His fist quickly flew into Colin's face.

The impact and the searing pain that Colin felt between his eyes caused his vision to temporarily black out. He stumbled back and fell against two chairs as he hit the floor. He could still hear the Lieutenant berating him.

"Those men that you and Driscol killed had friends here. Everyone's gonna want a piece of your ass."

Colin tried to stand as he felt several pairs of hands grab him from behind and pull him up. The men held his arms firmly behind his back. Colin imagined his enemies felt that he was helpless as they closed in. He could use his power to free himself all too easily. But he was adamant on his position. In spite of his impending fate these were men that he could not harm. One trooper raised his fist to strike a devastating blow onto Colin's face. As the burly fist rushed towards Colin a hand reached out and grabbed it in time to halt the connection. Diane had stepped in to prevent Colin from being lynched by these men.

"Step back," Diane's grim warning to the men.

The trooper struggled desperately against Diane's unyielding grip, only to submit to her power. His hand was firmly locked in place.

"Sergeant McKenzie is with me. You have a problem with him then maybe you can include me in your little discussion."

"Oh yeah? And just who the hell are you?" the Lieutenant demanded.

"Captain Christy," Diane stated with an air of pride.

There was silence among the men.

"That's Captain Diane Christy," Diane added. "Ace pilot. You might have heard of me. I've scored two hundred and thirty confirmed enemy kills."

Colin was in no mood to suffer through another session of ego polishing with Diane. "Lady, they don't know you. Just drop it."

"Captain Christy?" the Lieutenant skeptically inquired. "And just what are you to this freak?"

"Like I said. He's with me," Diane's reply. She shoved the trooper's arm away, easily sending him to the floor in the process.

"Maybe the Captain would want to watch who she associates with. Unless you already know that he's a murderer," the Lieutenant charged.

"All this is new to me," said Diane. "You might have the wrong person, so maybe you should let him go."

"Trust me. We have the right man. I was up close and personal when I saw him kill two of my men. I was even closer when he tried to kill me."

Diane turned her eyes to Colin. "Is this true?"

Colin hesitated for several seconds, ashamed to incriminate himself in this room full of silent people who were now focused on him. He grudgingly confessed. "I just now remembered. So I suppose it is."

For a minute Diane joined the silence in the room and stared at Colin. Colin was at least thankful that there was no anger on her face. No look of disgust.

"Let him go," Diane ordered the men.

"No damn way," the Lieutenant contested. "Maybe you didn't hear me. This man killed two of my men. He's a murderer and a traitor. We're taking him down."

"Maybe you made a mistake," Diane returned.

"It's no mistake, lady," the Lieutenant wailed in bewilderment. "I saw this son of a bitch kill two of my men. He shot one and burned the other. Then he tried to kill me. You think I imagined him shooting me four times?"

Diane continued staring at Colin. Colin felt as though her eyes were slicing away layers of his face in order to fully expose his cowering soul to every hostile person in the room.

"I'll deal with Sergeant McKenzie. Let him go," Diane told the men.

The Lieutenant continued to protest. "Let him go? No way, lady. He's not walking out of here."

Diane turned her eyes to the Lieutenant. "I'm giving you men a direct order to let the Sergeant go. If not then I'll have all of you charged with insubordination, assault and battery, inciting a riot, and whatever else I can find in the book. Or maybe you guys would like to take your little problem and deal directly with me."

Diane took a step towards the Lieutenant. Her tall stature with both her fists tightly clenched was an imposing sight that even gave Colin cause to shudder. Defying Diane would prove to be a grave mistake.

The Lieutenant stared back into Diane's determined, unsmiling face. Finally he grumbled a response. "Let him go."

The other men were slow to comply, but they released their hold on Colin and backed away from he and Diane.

The Lieutenant pointed his finger at Colin's face. "This is the second time you got your ass saved by the top brass, McKenzie. You must be leading a charmed life. But don't think that this is over."

With that warning the Lieutenant and his entourage stormed out of the cafeteria. Colin was now left with an even thicker cloak of uncertainty and confusion about his life. And the embarrassing pain that he felt after being assaulted twice by the man that he hoped to befriend was still burning. All eyes in the cafeteria were still affixed on him. He would endure no more of their judgmental stares. He quickly headed for the door.

"Hey Sarge, wait up," Diane called.

Colin ignored her. He shoved his way out of the door and walked towards the barracks where he was given a small room. So much for a perfect evening, thought Colin. He now planned to lay on his cot and brood.

"Sarge," Diane's voice called out from behind.

Colin was hoping that Diane would not follow him.

"Sergeant," Diane cried louder.

Colin continued walking, ignoring her.

"Colin," Diane shouted.

Colin decided to stop.

"You wanna tell me what the hell's going on," Diane demanded to know.

"Were you taking a nap back there and missed everything?" Colin bitterly admonished. "I killed a couple of their pals so now they're pissed off at me. Happens all the time."

"Did you really kill those guys?"

Colin turned to face Diane. "If I remember it then it's true."

Diane took a moment to ponder the truth that Colin relayed to her. "Maybe you had a good reason. I don't know. I wasn't there. But what I meant was why did you take all that crap from those goons?"

"What are you talking about?" Colin growled.

"I'm talking about the way that they swatted you around. Hell, they knocked you on your ass twice. They would have taken you apart if I hadn't stepped in. And you didn't do one damn thing to stop them."

"How was I supposed to stop them?" Colin impatiently groused. "You want me to use my power against men on our own side? It's obvious that I've already done enough damage."

"I'm not saying that you should become some kind of serial killer. I'm saying that you should have done something to defend yourself," Diane loudly exclaimed. "I don't understand you. You snub me to rush over to those knuckleheads. Then you let them walk all over you. Are you stupid or something?"

"No, I'm not," Colin snapped back. "I did what I did because those guys were part of my old squad and I don't have any friends. I was hoping to hook up with them and find out a little more about myself. Looks like I found a little more than I bargained for."

Colin noticed an immediate change in Diane's demeanor. Her mood switched from stern to disheartened. "That's very interesting. You don't have any friends. I don't have any friends either. That's why I sat at your table. I was hoping that we could open the curtain between us, just a little, and try to be friends."

There was a sadness in Diane's voice that Colin never expected to hear. At first he was annoyed by her presence. Now he felt guilty over being so openly intolerant towards her.

"I can see that I was just wasting my time," Diane sadly muttered. "Just as well. I'm an officer. A Captain. It doesn't look right for an officer to fraternize with the grunts."

"I didn't mean any harm by what I said," Colin told Diane.

Looking behind Diane Colin spotted another person that he did not expect to see. Blair Van Doren was heading this way. After enduring a horrendous evening like this Blair was the last person that Colin wanted to see now, if ever.

"Colin, Diane. I was trying to contact you both earlier," Blair told them. He smiled brightly. "What's going on?"

"Nothing, Doctor. I was just leaving," Diane said with a cold tone. "The Sergeant here can do whatever he wants."

Diane walked away, leaving Colin feeling even more guilty. He was so preoccupied with his personal insecurities that he failed to realize that Diane possessed a sensitive side that was capable of being hurt. Stupid move, Colin scolded himself. Now the wedge between he and Diane would certainly be driven deeper.

"What was that all about?" Blair asked.

"Just a little disagreement. Nothing that would concern you," was Colin's rude response.

"Maybe we should get her back and try to smooth things out."

"Colin balked at that idea. "Let her go. She wants to be alone. So do I,"

Colin turned his back to Blair and began to walk away.

"Hold on. Maybe we can sit and chat for a while."

Another idea that Colin quickly found distasteful. "I don't think so. Just leave me the hell alone."

Doctor Blair Van Doren. A person who's secrecy was partly responsible for the problems that Colin was facing. Colin was content with never seeing or speaking to Blair again in life, if not for the young man's stubborn insistence.

"Colin, wait up," Blair called. "If I've done anything to offend you then you can't keep it to yourself. Join me for dinner and we'll talk."

Colin ignored Blair and continued walking.

"I can answer a lot of questions. There are several important things that you should know."

Colin stopped. Now Blair had caught his interest. He turned back to face Blair. "You better make this good," his stern advise.

Colin followed Blair back into the cafeteria. Blair entered the line and picked up a tray to get served. Colin returned to the table where he previously sat. His tray was still there. His food had gotten cold. No matter, Colin was not hungry now. He was here to gain information from Blair. It took Blair a few minutes to get a full tray and sit down next to Colin.

"You're not hungry?" asked Blair.

"I already ate," Colin's somber reply.

Colin noticed that a few people were picking up their trays and walking over to a large video screen in the far corner. "Looks like it's time for the floor show," Blair commented to him.

At this time the Brelac regularly broadcast their propaganda transmissions to attempt to throw a scare into Protectorate troopers. The Brelac transmitted scenes of mutilated bodies scattered across a desolate landscape. Stacks of dead troopers being incinerated on a mass pyre. The smoldering ruins of cities and military bases. The scenes were narrated by the gravelly voice of an unnamed Brelac. His snarling face occasionally appeared on screen to predict that all Humans will soon die for the glory of the Brelac Empire.

Many troopers were unimpressed by the Brelac's threats. A few considered these videos to be more entertaining than demoralizing. Colin began watching them when he first started working here at Nocturne. In the beginning he was highly disturbed by them. But after gradually getting used to them he regarded them as pure propaganda. At the moment he was more interested in what Blair had to say. The transmission would be nothing that he had not heard before.

Blair nearly choked on a mouthful of chipped beef when he heard a familiar voice utter a light hearted, "Good evening." Blair bolted from his seat and rushed over to the small crowd gathered in front of the video screen.

Colin thought that this broadcast must be serious if it could pull Blair away from his meal so quickly. He joined Blair. Colin had no idea who he was watching, but Blair knew. His eyes widened in disbelief as they confronted the face that matched the voice. A man with long blond hair tied into a ponytail.

The man cheerfully introduced himself. "My name is Doctor Howard Fenlow. I'll be replacing your regular host for tonight's episode of total obliteration, courtesy of the Brelac Empire. For those of you who aren't familiar with me I used to work with the military on various projects. I stress the term, used to. I've recently decided to broaden my horizons and work with the Brelac to help bring an end to this pointless war."

"Fenlow, working with the Brelac? This has to be a ruse," a shocked Blair said in a barely audible voice.

Fenlow continued. "I'm not going to waste your time showing you any scenes of charred bodies or bloodied torture victims strapped to chairs. Instead I'm going to make this message as brief as possible. At this very moment the Brelac and I are on the verge of completing a weapon of devastating power. A weapon from which there will be no defense. It is not my wish to cause any unnecessary bloodshed. Therefore, on behalf of the Brelac Empire I am issuing an ultimatum. The United Protectorate has three days to order all military forces to disarm and surrender. I will personally guarantee the safety of any person who decides to cooperate."

A trooper standing next to Colin scoffed at Fenlow's promise. "A traitor guaranteeing our safety?"

"Three days should be enough time for you to contact all forces stationed throughout the quadrant. For everyone's sake I hope that President Drennen will have the courage to do the right thing and put an and to this war. There will be no other broadcasts made after this. Remember, three days."

The screen went dark. The message left Colin totally confused. He did not know what to make of this ultimatum delivered by a fellow Human. But he did recognize the man's name. "Doctor Howard Fenlow? Isn't he the man that you said can help us?" he inquired of Blair.

"It looks like Doctor Fenlow isn't planning to help anybody," Blair stated to his chagrin.

A trooper turned away from the screen, frowning in disaproval. "Who the hell was that guy giving ultimatums? Talks like he's somebody important."

"He was important," Blair muttered. "Now he's become somebody dangerous."

CHAPTER 11

▼

Carp Technologies enormous disk shaped starbase rested peacefully on the far outer fringes of Protectorate space. There was sparse traffic coming to and from the structure. Huge rectangular cargo vessels delivered their payloads collected from Carp's mining operations on distant moons. Small oval shaped shuttle craft transported work crews to and from Carp's lunar based research laboratories scattered throughout this region.

Since the start of the war Carp's starbase remained relatively safe, thanks to the graciousness of the Brelac. The starbase not only served as a corporate headquarters. It also housed over a dozen heavy manufacturing operations, as well as research and development laboratories. The starbase was also safe haven for five hundred of the company's technicians, scientists and executives. Carp's Chief Executive Officer also resided here, Walter Carnaby.

Carnaby was the only person traveling through this brightly lit corridor. His dark suit easily stood out against the light and white paneled walls. This entire section of the starbase was restricted to executive level personnel. A special meeting had been called by the other members of Carp's executive board. Carnaby expected the others to already be assembled in the main conference room. But he was in no hurry. One of the many small perks of his position was the ability to invoke patience in others. His subordinates can wait. No one was going anywhere. Not when he had the answers to all their questions.

The conference room door quietly slid open upon Carnaby's approach. Carnaby grinned at the sight of the seven executives seated at the round wooden table with it's polished surface. The grim frowns on the faces of these middle aged men seemed to be an extension of the dark suits and ties that they wore. These were the sullen faced managers of Carp's various operations. They were here to voice their concerns about Doctor Fenlow's ultimatum.

"Good afternoon, gentlemen," Carnaby's light hearted greeting. He sat down in his usual reserved seat.

At Carnaby's left was Rodger Bannister. A bespectacled man with receding black hair. He was Carp's director of security. At his right was a chubby man with curly brown hair. John Steiner. Carp's director of operations.

"I don't have to imagine why this meeting was requested. No doubt everyone here had heard Fenlow's little message to the government," Carnaby stated.

Bannister had a scathing opinion of Fenlow and his ultimatum. "We couldn't help hearing. It was on every damn wavelength. Video and audio. Who the hell does that idiot think he is? Shooting his mouth off, making such a demand. And with our preparations for Operation Broad Axe. He's sure to expose us."

"Not if we're careful," Carnaby's opinion. "Fenlow is probably acting on my orders. I instructed him to do whatever he could to advance our plan. Remember, we all mutually agreed that it would be prudent to move as quickly as possible. With the increased Brelac aggression and the gradual deterioration of the Protectorate military this ultimatum could work in our favor."

Steiner remained skeptical. "I fail to see how this can work to our advantage. If you ask me such a move will only serve to agitate the military. They'll be on a heightened state of alert."

"And what of it? Let them be on alert," replied Carnaby. "Fenlow will create an opening for us. One that will allow our operation to succeed with minimal difficulty. Trust me. Let's just wait and keep our eyes open."

"Have you had any contact with Fenlow?" Bannister asked.

"It's been a few days since I've personally spoken with him. And if he is working with the Brelac then I imagine that he'll be more difficult to reach. But I can afford to be patient. Somehow Fenlow will make contact when the time comes."

"When the time comes," Bannister grimly repeated. "That's what concerns me. What happens when the three days are up and the government doesn't surrender?"

Carnaby gave serious thought to that question. He knew that Fenlow would not make such a threat without the power to back it up. Fenlow mentioned that he and the Brelac were constructing a weapon of devastating power. He would most certainly be using the advanced psionic technology that he had developed. Carnaby was comfortable with Fenlow's intentions. Fenlow was using the Brelac to help pave the way for Operation Broad Axe. After the three day deadline it was possible that the final phase of the plan could finally get underway."

Carnaby firmly stated his position to the board. "When that time comes we take our opening."

"You sound so confident," Bannister jeered back. "That this small group can accomplish what thousands of heavily armed Vendetta troops failed to do. Overthrow the central government."

Carnaby laughed in contempt. "The fearsome hordes of Vendetta. Without our guidance and material support they would quickly revert back to splintered groups of right wing extremists venting their spleen at any suitable target. A more technically conceived plan is sure to succeed where lowbrow aggression has failed."

"Speaking of technical concepts, what about those three Reploids that were lost?" Steiner asked.

"They pose no threat," Carnaby simply stated. "The Reploids were to be diverted to Lodestar. Once they arrived our operative planned to keep them tied up with a battery of pointless tests and training exercises."

"Seems like a hell of a lot of trouble," Steiner scoffed. "It would have been easier to just kill them."

"I originally ordered them to be terminated, but the entire project was being watched too closely. We couldn't run the risk of raising any suspicions. The Reploids are now currently stationed at Nocturne on the planet Trillion. My intelligence reports that they spend their time serving in menial tasks."

"But what if the military decides to send them against us?" Bannister wondered.

"The military doesn't know about our activities or where to find us," Carnaby impatiently replied. "And if they were to pose a threat to us and our plans then I'm placing my trust in Fenlow to deal with them."

"Fenlow and the Brelac," Bannister reminded Carnaby.

"Do you still think that we can trust the Brelac?" Steiner asked Carnaby.

"Trust doesn't matter. Only their usefulness. Don't forget that after the success of this operation no force will be able to pose a threat to us. And the entire United Protectorate will at last be in our rightful control."

CHAPTER 12

▼

Deep within Rantraven base Mariner was enjoying a little rest and recreation in his quarters. He was seated at a small round table with his faithful confidant, Senior General Owen Lagar. They were absorbed by a centuries old game that consisted of a multicolored board with cards, dice and tiny plastic houses. It was an economic game involving the principles of buying and selling. Two forces working to amass wealth and resources until one gained sufficient power to ruin the other. It was a game that Mariner's Brelac mind could perfectly relate to. It's name, Monopoly.

Lagar often joined Mariner for these gaming sessions. Since Mariner hand picked Lagar as his second in command the two were rarely far apart. Mariner valued Lagar's military mind. They shared a mutual brilliance and a love of warfare. Together they executed many successful military campaigns to expand the power of the Brelac empire. Like Mariner Lagar was a strict disciplinarian and a rigid perfectionist. Mariner demanded no less than total efficiency from his subordinates. Overseeing all military operations it was Lagar's job to see that Mariner's directives were carried out without any deviation.

The competitive amusement and relaxation in these lavish quarters were just one of many perks that Mariner enjoyed as the supreme leader of the Brelac empire. His quarters were dimly lit, yet elegantly decorated rooms that looked as though they were taken from a page out of late twentieth century Earth history. The floor was covered by brown linoleum tiles. The walls were paneled with a dark wood that was polished to a near reflective shine. In the middle of the room hung a chandelier with dozens of polished crystal droplets. Standing against the walls were several antique wooden chairs and tables that were assembled by skilled carpenters. These quarters were temporary and beautifully furnished, but not as large or decorous as the Commander's Palace back on Old Earth. But still, until Mariner brought the war in this sector to a victorious conclusion he was content to call these quarters home.

Mariner was about to take a roll of the dice. He was distracted by a series of loud beeps coming from a small monitor on a nearby table. Mariner cursed aloud. There was a transmission coming in. The face of Doctor Fenlow appeared on screen.

"Have you heard any word from my government?" Fenlow inquired.

Mariner ignored Fenlow for the moment. Lagar also remained silent. Mariner rolled the dice across the game board that was faded yellow with age. They landed with two fives face up. Mariner's taloned fingers clumsily moved a small metal figurine of a thimble across ten spaces on the board. He landed on Baltic Avenue, a space that he had already owned and had a green house on. With his turn completed Mariner diverted his attention to Fenlow's remarks. "No word yet," he croaked in his deep and gruff voice.

"I didn't think so," said Fenlow. "Perhaps I've underestimated their tenacity when I issued that ultimatum. It would appear that they're not going to lay down and surrender because of just another transmitted threat. Even if the format suddenly changed and it featured a Human face."

"They've still got two days left. I'm in a good enough mood to give your people the benefit of the doubt," Mariner replied.

"Patience and restraint from a Brelac? You really must be light hearted right now," stated a surprised Fenlow. "Perhaps at the start of the war we could have ordered Protectorate troopers to play polka music and juggle knives to keep you Brelac amused. It might have saved a lot of bloodshed. But it the meantime I have work to get back to. I'll leave you to your recreation."

Finally Fenlow mentioned something that drew Mariner's interest. "I'm glad that you mentioned your work, Doctor. I'm anxious to receive a status report on this grand project Viperhawk that I'm helping to support."

"I'm running a series of final checks on the Viperhawk's systems. My ultimatum transmission was simply one test that I've conducted. I estimate that it will be another few days before I can execute a final test run. I'll keep you posted as things develop."

Mariner's mouth widened into a toothy smile. "Fine. If you need anything then don't hesitate to ask."

Mariner's smile was still beaming at Fenlow when the screen went black. Mariner imagined that Fenlow could not suspect the level of duplicity that was hiding behind that smile.

Now that Fenlow was gone Mariner's smile immediately faded. As did the patience that he openly displayed. "I look forward to the day when our relationship with that man becomes redundant."

Lagar shared Mariner's sediments. "I can't wait to be rid of him either. And his masters at Carp. Who the hell does he think he is making an ultimatum like that without consulting us first? And it continuously irks me that these Humans were able to make such a quantum improvement on our technology."

"The advanced Reploids," Mariner nodded. "His work is highly impressive. Our experiments in giving our soldiers advanced psionic powers through their implants have had little success. The huge surge of psionic energy always destroys the subjects nervous systems. The experiments were always one hundred percent fatal to the test subjects. But Fenlow has found a way around that problem. His subjects have an engineered gene that enables their nervous tissue to rapidly regenerate. Rather than have our own technicians try to duplicate Fenlow's work I think that it's better to bide our time and get everything we can out of him and Carp. Then he'll become expendable."

Now it was Lagar's turn to smile. "I can hardly wait. For that moment to come. I suppose I'll just have to wait until this project Viperhawk of his is completed before I can act."

"It's fortunate that he shared all his data. Especially his process for creating rapidly grown in-vitro reploids to Major Danton. Plus that method that he uses to program their minds. Fenlow's methods are far more advanced than our own cloning techniques. He may be putting a lot of faith in this Viperhawk project, but his cloning process is the real gem. Think of it. We have the superior technology to cut a path of conquest wherever we go. But there's only one major problem that we have to face."

"The manpower," Lagar quickly replied. "There's only a few million of us. If we want to take on the entire universe we'd be stretched out pretty thin."

"Exactly. We need a hell of a lot more personnel if we want to take on some of the endeavors that I have planned. Despite our efforts and technology we can't create a faster way to develop in-vitro cloned organisms. But Fenlow has. Rather than waiting for about sixteen years or so for our clones to reach maturity we can use Fenlow's method and grow them in a matter of days. And program them quickly. That will cut down on the time used to educate and train them for military service. And if we can give them some of the special psionic abilities that he gave those new advanced Reploids then that will be a huge bonus."

"Our military power will increase a hundred fold," said Lagar. "After we get the United Protectorate worlds under control we can start a mass cloning and construction program. We can turn entire star systems into massive factories. Cranking out troops, ships and equipment. Then when we're ready to make our move nothing can stand against us. All with the help of the soon to be departed Doctor Fenlow."

CHAPTER 13

▼

The gargantuan orb, Starbase Twelve drifted in a silent orbit high above the planet Morthos Three. Among the many Brelac ships that were docked here there was one that Doctor Fenlow had converted into his immediate base of operations. The Viperhawk, a dark oval shaped battle cruiser with broad swept forward wings folded against it's side to allow the ship to dock. At the ship's nose dozens of spider-like construction drones floated about like a swarm of bees. The drones were equipped with eight telescoping arms with dexterous pinchers. Several drones carried panels of transparent crystal. Other drones assisted them as they interlocked these panels of crystal together on the nose of the ship. Molecular bonding tools at the end of their arms fused each panel seamlessly together.

Inside the Viperhawk it's brightly lit corridors were empty. There were no Brelac crewmen manning their stations. Fenlow was sitting at a metal table in a large circular room. He was jotting down a few notes. Then he rose up and headed for a six foot column shaped device in the center of the room. There was a keyboard installed on the side of the column. This device was a specially designed computer system that Fenlow had created. A powerful computer enhanced by living brain tissue that Fenlow had cloned and rapidly grew in the incubation tube back at the laboratory in Rantraven. The tissue itself was enhanced by larger versions of Fenlow's psionic implants. Within the computer's housing the large mass of cerebral matter rested inside a life support container. It was constantly fed oxygen and a nutrient fluid while it was connected to the computer hardware below.

All of the Viperhawk's functions were maintained by this computer. No crew was needed. Instead of the bridge this circular room was the ship's nerve center.

Fenlow was confident that this computer could operate every function within this ship far more quickly and efficiently than any living crew. For a personal touch Fenlow could not resist granting the computer a name, Succubus.

Fenlow pressed a sequence of keys on the keyboard to summon data on the ship's status. The crisp telepathic image of the ship's schematics appeared above the keyboard. Fenlow liked what he was seeing. Succubus' control of the ship's entire propulsion system was now flawless. Fenlow nodded in silent approval.

The door behind Fenlow slid open. Major Danton entered the room. "Still no reply from your people?"

"Not even an invitation to go to hell," replied Fenlow. "I don't expect them to send an answer tomorrow either. But still, it was a perfect way to test Succubus' communications capability. President Drennen and the others would be amazed to know that they had received a message transmitted telepathically over the gulf of space."

Danton scoffed. "I still think that it was a waste of energy. And an unauthorized waste of energy at that. You should have cleared it with Mariner or General Lagar first."

"I saw no need, considering the fact that Mariner himself placed me in full charge of this project," Fenlow calmly rebuked.

"If you say so," Danton ceded. "But I am curious to know what you intend to do if your people refuse to surrender. Do you intend to take on the entire Protectorate military by yourself?"

A sinister grin appeared on Fenlow's face. "In a way, yes," He turned back to the computer. "Succubus."

Above the computer's column form the image of a large eye surrounded by pulsating cerebral matter appeared. This self image was another personalizing touch that Fenlow had given the computer.

Fenlow issued his orders. "Contact Captain Stergis at Rantraven's robotics research lab. Tell him that I need the Cybernoids transported here at once."

"The Cybernoids?" asked Danton.

"Yes. The Cybernoids will carry out my retaliation. I designed them as a counterforce against the Reploids. Now would be the perfect time to use them."

"I hope that you're planning to seek Mariner's approval for this," Danton stated.

"You're free to consult Mariner and tell him whatever you want. My only concern is the success of this experiment."

"An expensive experiment," Danton returned, showing skepticism over the idea. "If you send these Cybernoids out to find the Reploids then they might wind up fighting an army of Protectorate troopers at the same time. I would be more confident if you had built more than just three of them. They won't be able to stand up to any sizable force."

Fenlow scoffed at Danton's opinion. "You'll change your mind about my Cybernoids after they win their first battle. Have you forgotten that I've incorporated my psionic technology into their construction? They're part machine, part living organisms. Their psionically based weapons systems make them more powerful than a battle cruiser. Their sensors are twice as powerful and accurate than anything you currently possess. I can always construct more Cybernoids but for now these three alone will be enough to get the job done."

"I hope you're right," Danton's response. "But if they should find where the Reploids are stationed then they must report their position to central command. We'll send out a strike force to aid them in dealing with any enemy resistance."

Fenlow suspected that Danton wanted to barge in on the operation and claim some credit for himself if there was a successful attack. That was of no consequence. Let the fool join in on the fun and games if he wanted to, thought Fenlow. "If you feel that it's necessary to send in some troops then I won't argue with you. But I'm confident that the Cybernoids will easily handle any resistance."

Danton nodded in satisfaction. "Fine. Meanwhile, I've received word from Captain Armatage back on Rantraven. His genetics research section is working to create our own Reploid production program. He's following your formula for the nutrient liquid."

"Yes, the nutrient. The key to accelerating their growth and development. Without the nutrient you'll have to wait several years instead of a few days for the organisms to safely mature. And don't forget the neural gene. Without it the Reploids won't survive more than a week with their increased psionic powers."

"I also came to report that the Viperhawk's forward lens array will be completed in two hours. We're going through a lot of trouble to make everything to your specifications. That lens installation, the computer hardware. We even donated this ship to your project. It's fairly new. Only saw two battles since it left the shipyard. I hope that this project of yours is worth all the hype that you gave us."

Fenlow stated with full confidence, "I've already bet my life on it's success. Since the lens array will be completed soon then perhaps we can drop another unexpected surprise on our friends."

CHAPTER 14

▼

Colin, Kelly and Blair were seated at an oblong table in a conference room. Colin sat nervously while imagining several reasons why he and the others were assembled here. Diane was also summoned but had yet to arrive. All they were told was that General Larkin needed to speak to them about an urgent matter. Kelly, sitting at Colin's right remained quiet while nervously biting his thumbnail. An equally silent Blair sat across from Colin. Colin was not focused on whatever Larkin's problem could be. His current thoughts were concentrated on the fiasco that he called a life. He was mystified that no one else knew of him. His entire past was still a dark shroud covering a brick wall. He was also terrified at the thought of what might be waiting for him behind that same wall. He was still shocked at the revelation that he had killed two men and tried to kill Lieutenant Yates. This caused him to wonder if he had committed any other atrocities in his dark past.

During these past two days Colin could still not locate any old friends from his past. He still could not summon any names to follow. This lead to his latest failure to track down any known relatives. Colin now felt that his frustration over this matter had reached it's end. The possible base to this puzzle was sitting at this table across from him, Blair Van Doren. After this meeting concludes Colin planned to dog Blair until he finally surrendered some satisfactory answers.

"How have you been sleeping?" Kelly asked Colin.

"How have I been sleeping?" Colin returned. "Why are you asking?"

"Just wondering. I have these dreams. They're pretty vivid. I find myself replaying my day's activities. What I've done and who I've talked to. I dream about it all night. Occasionally I'll see you, Diane or Blair in my place. Following my routine. It's the same thing every night."

"I have those same dreams," Colin exclaimed with surprise. He turned to Blair for an answer. "Does this mean anything?"

Blair calmly explained, "It could be stress connected with your jobs. It's possible that you've been concentrating too much displeasure on your work. Your subconscious minds are replaying your activities in your sleep."

Colin felt that Blair's reasoning was highly dubious. The format of these dreams were too systematic to be just a vexation over work coming back to haunt both he and Kelly. He wondered if Diane was having the same dreams as well.

The door to the conference room slid open and Diane strode in.

"Hello Diane," Blair cheerfully greeted.

"Doctor," Diane returned. She walked around the table and sat down next to Blair.

Blair was the only one who acknowledged Diane. She said nothing to Colin or Kelly. She sat quietly and stared down at the table.

The conference room door slid open again. This time General Larkin entered. Colin joined the others in unison as they jumped to their feet and stood at attention.

"Please be seated," Larkin told the group. "I'm glad to see you all here. Sorry that we couldn't meet under happier circumstances. But as you know we have an urgent situation on our hands. Undoubtably you've heard that one of our top scientists, Doctor Howard Fenlow. has apparently defected to the Brelac and issued an ultimatum on their behalf. He claims that he can give them the power to win the war overnight."

"What does that have to do with us, sir?" Colin asked.

"I was hoping that you could tell me," Larkin returned. "It's likely that Fenlow is working on some new weapon's project with the Brelac. The three of you are Fenlow's creations. You might have some knowledge of what he's doing. And with your powers you might be able to find some way to stop him."

Colin felt that Larkin was grasping at straws. There was little that he, Diane and Kelly could do against such an unknown menace. But still, Colin did not want to disappoint Larkin. "We'll be glad to help out in any way we can, sir."

Diane raised her hand to grab Colin's attention. "Excuse me, Sarge. Any idea how we're gonna pull this off?" she asked. There was a heavy tone of sarcasm in her voice. "Maybe you can share your game plan with the rest of us."

To Colin's chagrin he now felt guilty about voicing a commitment to the General without consulting the others. Still, he maintained a calm composure and sought to save face by devising a crude plan of action. "Undoubtably Fenlow is now under the protection of the Brelac. He won't be easy to reach. Were you able to trace his transmission?"

Larkin explained, "The previous ultimatums were sub space transmissions traced to an unknown source in the Dione system. That's deep within Brelac territory. Now Fenlow's transmission is a total mystery. The previous transmissions were received on a specific frequency. Fenlow's transmission was received on every frequency imaginable. Video and audio. Military and civilian. It broke into every transmission all the way back to Maseklos Prime. Even though it was such a powerful transmission all attempts to trace it have failed. It was as if the transmission came from nowhere."

"Maybe it's possible to retrace Fenlow's steps," Colin suggested. "We can search his home and his workplace to get a clue on what he was working on. Possibly find out how he was able to contact the Brelac."

"That will be easier said than done," Larkin replied. "His apartment and lab back on Maseklos Prime were already searched. There was nothing out of the ordinary. And his associates and superiors at Carp Technologies offered very little information."

A sudden high pitched wail filled the room and caught everyone by unaware. Colin saw worried looks appear on Larkin and Blair's faces.

"The emergency alarm," said Blair. "The base must be under attack."

A shrill beep sounded out from Larkin's coat. "What now?" he muttered in frustration. He took a small cellular communicator out of his hip pocket. He pressed a button on the communicator and spoke. "Larkin here. What's going on?"

The look on Larkin's face changed from distress to confusion as he listened to the report. He shared the grim details to Colin and the others. "The command center reports that we are indeed under attack. So far we've suffered heavy casualties. We've lost a full battalion of troopers and a dozen hovertanks."

"The Brelac must have a couple of divisions out there," was Blair's theory.

"It's just three," said Larkin.

"Three divisions?" Asked Blair

"Three units," Larkin corrected. "Sounds incredible, but that's what all reports have stated. Three robots of some sort. I'm told that they're massively powerful. I was also told that there's a large force of Brelac air and ground units heading this way. They'll be here in twenty minutes."

"If we're under attack then you'd better get to safety, sir," Blair quickly warned Larkin.

"Don't worry about me. I escaped the fall of Helios," Larkin assured him. "I've escaped far worse situations during the course of my career."

For a moment Larkin was silent. Looking into the faces of Colin, Kelly and Diane. "Silencers Squad has been inactive for far too long. I'm putting the three of you back in action. I want you to go out, assess this robotic threat and deal with it as needed. I'll be in the command center monitoring the situation."

Colin joined Diane and Kelly in an enthusiastic, "Yes sir." Colin could not help noticing the broad smile that illuminated Diane's face. He wondered if she could see past her zeal for combat to appreciate the seriousness of what was going on. For Kelly and Blair it was a different matter. The worried frowns on their faces revealed their true feelings. Apprehension at the idea of facing an unknown and powerful enemy. Colin was also fearful of confronting whatever was waiting outside. Moments ago he was distributing supplies in a quiet, leaky supply room. Moments from now he will be in combat against an enemy that has decimated a battalion of troopers and twelve hovertanks. Colin may have been joyful over being returned to his rightful place, a member of a team going into battle. But his heart was pounding so heavily that he could not distinguish his excitement over his fear.

Colin and the others rose from their seats and followed Larkin out of the room.

CHAPTER 15

▼

On the outskirts of Nocturne Colin saw that a full scale battle was viciously raging. The might of Nocturne's forces were assembled to repel the enemy invaders. Scores of troopers were present and were firing every weapon from laser and plasma arms to portable missile launchers. Dozens of imposing hovertanks glided out and launched their devastating firepower against the enemy. But so far all of their efforts were proving to be futile against the advancing enemy. An incredible invading force of only three.

From out of a wall of fire and a cloud of dust and smoke emerged a trio of tall metallic humanoid creatures. They marched through powerful explosions while countless energy bolts bounced off of their bodies. Both without causing so much as the slightest blemish to these creatures. They towered seven feet above their Human foes. Their heads were large and bulbulous. Their only facial features were a thin horizontal lens serving as an eye. A thin vertical slit ran below the eye lens. Overall, their bodies were thick in build. They were broad chested with massive arms and legs that were certainly as powerful as they appeared.

They continued to advance with impunity through the Human assault without slowing their pace. They were completely impervious to firepower from the smaller arms. Colin wondered how these metallic creatures could stand up to a heavy barrage from the many hovertanks that were gathered here. As far as Colin could see the robots advance was a passive one. They were allowing the troopers to do all the shooting. The robots spread out, then stopped before the small army of troopers that were still blazing away at them with intense fury.

One of the robots raised it's hands towards a hovertank that was about to fire at it. The robot fired twin beams of crimson energy from it's palms that demolished the vehicle in a thundering blast. It's two companions followed suit and fired their energy beams at tanks and troopers alike. The troopers began to scatter while being battered by this assault. A group of fighters flew over Colin and the others at a low altitude. Colin watched the fighters close in on the robotic invaders for a frontal assault. No doubt the fighters were launched from Nocturne's air base. There were ten of them. Colin wondered if this number would be enough to accomplish the task of destroying the robots.

The fighters plasma cannons blazed away at the robots. A large panel of energy that resembled smoky glass instantly appeared in front of each robot. The devastating firepower from the fighters was easily absorbed by these shields. The metal creatures behind them were perfectly safe.

As the fighters soared overhead the shields disappeared. The robots quickly turned and sent out a hail of their potent energy bolts at the aircraft. The robot's aim was as reliable as ever. In a single strike all but two of the fighters were blasted out of the sky. Regrouping to stage another attack the troopers found that the robot's horizontal lens eye also served an offensive purpose. One of the robots fired a crimson beam of energy in the midst of several charging Humans. The luckier victims were reduced to ashes in a split second. The less fortunate ones were instantly transformed into walking torches. They flailed about in minutes of agony before they fell to the ground and perished.

As the three robots continued to scorch the area with their heat rays Human casualties mounted. Suddenly Colin spotted a swarm of black stingray shaped fighter craft making a rapid approach.

"Incoming! Take cover!" Colin shouted. These stingray fighters were obviously part of the invasion force that Larkin warned about. Before Colin and the others could run for cover the fighters soared overhead without strafing the area. They ignored the activity taking place on the ground and headed for the base.

Several troopers now began to fall back from the battle with the robots. One trooper approached Colin's group. "We've been ordered to retreat. We can't hold these things back, let alone the Brelac ground troops heading this way. The entire base is being evacuated."

Colin absorbed the grim report but was not prepared to accept defeat so soon. "Those things will reach the base before any Brelac troops. We're going to have to deal with them. Maybe help buy some time for the evacuation."

"Suit yourself," the trooper replied. Then quickly ran off.

"Let him go," Said Diane. She walked over to a dead trooper laying on his back. She stripped a laser pistol and gun belt from the body. After quickly strapping the belt around her waist she commandeered his AR-20 rapid mortar rifle. A cumbersome weapon with a long barrel and a large magazine on the top.

Diane seemed to be just as eager to get into this fight as ever. Colin observed Kelly's face. His skin was pale. His hands were shaking. Indications that he remained apprehensive about facing this powerful enemy. Colin sympathized with Kelly's fears. But if they possessed these arcane abilities then they had to put them to use and try to defeat this trio of robotic monsters. At least Colin was thankful that Blair reluctantly agreed to remain in the base. This was a dangerous situation. Without the benefit of special abilities Blair was certain to be the most vulnerable target and the first casualty.

Colin, Diane and Kelly advanced towards the robots. They each split up to face their opponent. Diane charged in to attack one of the robots. Her rapid mortar rifle spat out a burst of four explosive shells with a loud boom. Each shell that she fired exploded on the robot's body but left it unharmed. Diane fired a second burst but this one was also ineffective. Finally she tossed the rifle aside and charged towards the robot. She intended to replace her weapon with a closer hands on approach.

Diane sprinted towards the robot, but did not move fast enough. The robot thrust it's hand out and smashed it's palm into Diane's face. Diane was knocked senseless. Her nose was bloodied.

Diane was too dazed to defend herself. The robot's massive hand engulfed her head and prepared to crush it into a bloodied gel. Kelly moved quickly to intervene, sending a burst of fiery energy that struck the robot directly into it's face. The attack caused no damage but did serve to distract the monster from killing Diane. The robot turned to face Kelly. Kelly fired another stream of energy at the robot. Then he witnessed the futility of this action. The energy bounced harmlessly off of the robot's metallic skin. The robot responded by throwing Diane at Kelly. Her body sped through the air and slammed into Kelly with a force that rendered him unconscious.

As Diane and Kelly lay on the ground Colin watched the robot approach their immobile bodies. The two other robots were steadily closing in on his position as well. Colin decided to see if these machines could withstand a few thousand volts of electric current. Before Colin could put his plan into action one of the robots fired an energy bolt that exploded near his feet. The power of the blast threw Colin onto his back. He experienced a sudden throbbing in his head. Sparks leaped up from his hands. Streams of current flowed across the ground. Then the ground beneath Colin quickly sank to form a gaping crevasse that threatened to swallow him.

Colin desperately bore his fingers into the ground and hung onto the very edge of the crevasse. While he tried to climb out his head continued to throb. The crevasse continued to grow wider and longer. When the throbbing in Colin's head abruptly stopped the progression of the crevasse also halted. Colin was certain that the ground trying to swallow him was a bizarre manifestation of his power. Colin felt that if he only had conscious control over it, preferably within the next five seconds, then he could turn this new ability into a very useful weapon.

Colin turned and saw a small band of troopers charging in to make another assault on the robots. Their weapons blazed furiously but their efforts were being wasted. The countless laser and plasma bolts that they fired caused no damage to the robots. The troopers did buy Colin enough time to pull himself out of the crevasse while the robot's attention was diverted from him. Colin crawled beneath the wave of energy bolts until he was a safe distance away from the battle zone. He prepared to make another attack on a robotic target. This time hoping that his second attempt at destroying the machine would not be as disastrous as the first.

Colin generated a potent charge and raised his hands to release it towards one of the robots. The robot quickly raised it's hands in response. The intense blue flash of Colin's electrical bolt filled the air. The energy struck it's intended target but was absorbed into the robot's right hand. Another bolt of electricity was fired from the robot's left hand and struck Colin directly in his chest. Colin was unprepared to receive this sudden shock to his system. The charge lifted him off his feet and hurled him to the ground. The robot had effectively routed Colin's electrical charge through it's body and discharged it back to him. It was a highly effective tactic that left Colin flat on his back with a burning pain in his chest. He tried to rise but the pain increased with his movements. The robot advanced towards Colin. It stood over him ominously and raised it's hand. Looking up at the robot Colin knew that he was at the total mercy of this creature. At this range one of it's powerful energy blasts fired into his helpless form would reduce him to burning shards.

A barrage of laser bolts suddenly pelted the robot's face. Colin turned to catch a glimpse of the shooter. To his surprise Blair was standing several yards away with a laser rifle in his hands. Colin groaned in loud frustration. Blair was the last person that he wanted out here. Despite their paranormal abilities Silencers Squad horrendously bungled the attack against these robotic menaces. Blair's presence would only provide them with another victim to slaughter.

A group of hovertanks roared up and began firing their huge laser cannons at the robots. The robots reacted quickly, erecting their panels of protective shielding to absorb the tanks firepower. The tanks fired repeatedly at their targets, but their persistence was rewarded with total destruction. While the robot's shields protected them their powerful energy bolts quickly wore down the tank's protective shields. Then they began to demolish the tanks one by one.

While the robots attention were diverted to the hovertanks Colin struggled to withstand the searing pain in his chest and rise to his feet. He sprinted towards Blair, hoping to reach the young man before one of these hostile robots killed them both. A huge shadow suddenly fell over Colin. He stopped in his tracks and looked up to see a large ship hovering in the sky above him. It's two forward wings, folded against it's long oval body were spreading out. Long silvery rod projections extended from the tips of the wings. Colin cringed when he saw multiple openings appear underneath the ship to reveal numerous gun turrets. All pointed in his direction.

This was truly the end, thought Colin. Between this enemy ship above him and those robots he could not imagine any thoughts of survival. He closed his eyes and instinctively threw his hands in front of his face. As if the frail barriers of flesh and bone would serve as an adequate shield. Colin heard the sounds of rapid shooting. Screams rang out all around him. He opened his eyes and saw the gun turrets spitting out multiple laser bolts that dismembered dozens of troopers who were still in the area. Colin was shocked to learn that his life was spared. He also wondered if this act of mercy was some error on the Brelac's behalf. Whether this was a mistake or a stroke of blind luck Colin knew that he would have limited time to capitalize upon it.

A small group of fighters came soaring in to attack the large ship. A thick barrage of fire from the enemy vessel accurately destroyed the fighters instantly. Colin had seen enough of this ship. He ran to join Blair.

Colin was quick to scold Blair. "What the hell are you doing out here? I thought we agreed that you'd stay inside."

"And if I did you'd be dead by now," Blair countered in anger. "I'm more than capable of taking care of myself. I am a trained soldier, as well as a doctor."

"That will make one hell of an obituary," Colin fumed. He saw several more stingray fighters flying overhead. The large ship simply hovered silently. It's presence serving as a dreaded omen. "We'd better grab Diane and Kelly and get out of here. This fight is getting way over our heads."

Colin and Blair charged over to the spot where Diane and Kelly were laying. They were both still unmoving. Blair kneeled down to pick up Diane. He slung her across his back and proceeded to run towards the base. Colin was grateful that Blair was carrying the larger and heavier Diane. Kelly was smaller and would be easier to carry. He scooped up Kelly's limp body and held him with both arms. He sped off to catch up with Blair, dragging Kelly's feet across the ground.

Colin looked up and saw several fighters soaring overhead. They were being closely pursued by a group of stingray fighters. He looked back towards the three robots. They had effectively destroyed the last of the hovertanks that were plaguing them. The idea of taking these creatures on again was out of the question. They were too powerful while he, Diane and Kelly were far too disorganized. They were lucky to survive the first encounter against these machines. A second battle would be a death sentence. As much as Colin hated to turn and run his sense of self preservation prevailed. He conceded the victory of this battle to the enemy. But he promised himself that in the future the situation would be reversed. Next time Silencers Squad would not run.

CHAPTER 16

▼

Colin quickly caught up to Blair as they merged with a large mass of troopers that were ordered to retreat. Kelly had regained consciousness and was moving on his own. Blair still carried Diane's unconscious body across his back. The mob flowed through the open gate of the tall chain link fence that surrounded Nocturne's large airbase. All the fighters had launched to engage the invaders. The only ships remaining were small shuttles and cargo ships. Colin looked about to see if he could locate any available shuttle that could fly he and his friends out of here as quickly as possible. Everywhere Colin turned he witnessed scenes of utter chaos. Panicking mobs were fighting tooth and nail to board every ship that he saw. Troopers were desperately trying to coordinate the evacuation in the smoother and faster way that they were trained. The terrified masses were employing a different procedure to remove themselves out of harm's way. Board any ship quickly and every man for himself. Colin led the way, trying to find a ship where there were less people fighting to board it.

Shoving his way through a mad crush of shouting people he came upon a squadron of small ships that were being prepared for immediate departure by the flight crews. Colin spotted a small wedge shaped craft that looked as though it was barely large enough to carry the entire group. And there was no crowd fighting to board it. It was a scout craft. The hatch on the side of the ship was gaping wide open. Colin thought that this was perfect. They now had a ship ready to fly as soon as they boarded it.

Colin led the others up through the hatch and into the interior of the craft. He expected to find the pilot waiting inside the cockpit but the seat was empty. Colin sat down in the pilot's seat and strapped himself in. Blair gently pushed

Diane into the tiny space. Colin felt a sharp pain in his left shoulder as Diane's head pressed firmly against him. Blair squeezed himself in next, laying on top of Diane. In order for Kelly to fit inside he was forced to lay his body across Blair. Half of his torso came to rest in the cockpit, and over Colin's head. His face was mashed against the window. Colin had to lean forward to try and provide more room for Kelly, at the expense of his own comfort.

Colin found himself before a wide panel of intimidating buttons, L. E. D gauges and twin control sticks. Even without the small and uncomfortably tight confines of this ship studying these controls would be a difficult task.

Blair's frustrated voice broke Colin's train of thought. "Colin, this is not going to work. Let's try and board one of the other ships."

Colin quickly scoffed at that suggestion. "You saw those mobs out there. We'd never be able to board any of those ships. We were lucky to get this one to ourselves."

Kelly added his reservations to Blair's. "At least the people out there will be getting seats. And since when are you a pilot?"

"Since you two are laying on top of our real pilot, who happens to be out of it at the moment," Colin grumbled back.

Colin continued his attempt to decipher the ship's controls so that he could launch the ship. After a minute he gave up and decided to put what little knowledge that he had into operation. He thought that flying this ship should not be too hard. The engines were already on. All he had to do was put them in drive and manipulate the twin control sticks. He began pressing several buttons and switches but yielded no result. A little more exploring would be in order before this ship could take off.

Colin heard a faint sound rising up from the pile of bodies behind him. It was a muffled voice. "Sounds like Diane is waking up," he said. If Diane was regaining consciousness then it was certain that she would be confused by her new surroundings.

"Where the hell am I?" Diane's voice cried out. "I can't breathe!"

"We're all inside a coffin that's about to be launched into space," Kelly returned.

"We boarded a ship," Colin's accurate reply. "We're getting out of here."

"We're leaving?" asked Diane. "What about the fight?"

"We lost," Colin's blunt reply. "It was quick and embarrassing. Now we're getting out of here before it becomes lethal. I'm shutting the door."

. Colin located and pressed the switch on the panel that operated the hatch. The thick metal door slid itself shut with an airtight seal. Colin politely asked Kelly, "Excuse me. Can you push those buttons over there at your left?"

"What buttons?" Kelly shouted.

"They're at your left. Just below your neck. I can't reach them with you in the way. Unless Blair can reach them."

"Reach them?" Blair cried in disbelief. "I can't even see them."

"Never mind," Colin moaned in frustration. He contorted his body under Kelly to reach the desired buttons. He hoped that pressing them blindly would cause no serious harm.

The buttons that Colin pressed were the ones that switched the ship's engines out of their neutral position and into a drive function. The ship suddenly lurched forward, scraping against the ground and out of control. It's pilot, Colin, was crouched under Kelly and was away from the control sticks. When he rose up he looked through the ship's window to see dozens of troopers diving in every direction to avoid being mowed down. The ship was barreling on a collision course with a grounded shuttle. Colin grasped the control sticks and pulled them back. The ship bolted sharply into the air and passed over the shuttle. Colin had saved the ship from certain destruction, but the fact still remained that he was no pilot. With the control sticks in his unsteady hands he was now sending the ship spiraling wildly into the air.

The ship crashed into a lighting tower, ripping it apart. Then it climbed into the sky. Colin wondered if he would unintentionally do the job of killing the group instead of the Brelac. Now the trip was about to get even more dangerous. Protectorate and Brelac fighters were engaged in furious dogfights. Colin faced the risk of being hit by a stray shot or crashing into one of the other ships. Colin surprised himself by slipping the scout craft through the battle without suffering a scratch. The ship began to weave and spin under an unsteady control. Colin was in a state of panic. He began probing the instrument panel to find any control that would help him to stabilize the ship.

The wild ride was a most unpleasant experience for Colin. He felt as if his stomach were being turned inside out. In his nauseous and dizzy state he noticed the small monitor on the instrument panel. The ship's scanner. It showed a triangle representing the scout craft being chased by three oval shaped objects. The scanner's voice system activated itself and warned Colin that the ship was being pursued by the Brelac.

"Three enemy fighters are approaching from coordinates one, zero, one, two. They are rapidly closing in."

Colin's job as pilot was getting harder. "One, zero, one, two? Where the hell is that?" he screamed to the instrument panel.

"It's someplace we have to get away from," Blair's voice warned. "Far away."

Colin was still struggling to comprehend the controls before him. The control sticks were his greatest obstacles. He was unable to hold the control sticks steady and fly the ship on a straight course. Through the window he saw that the ship was still ascending into space. That came as a relief. Then he saw plasma bolts blazing past the ship.This was a highly intimidating sight. Colin knew that if one of those bolts struck this small ship it would mean instantaneous obliteration for everyone.

"Are they still on us?" Diane asked.

Colin glanced at the monitor. "As far as I can tell they're still on us."

"Why don't you turn and fight?"

Colin gave out a burst of laughter at such an impossible suggestion. "You want me to fight? I can't even fly this damn thing."

"Well then, flying lesson's over, Sarge. I'm taking over before you get us all killed," Diane firmly exclaimed.

Colin was all too happy to comply. The only problem was squeezing both their bodies inside this tight space in order to switch positions. Colin released the control sticks to try and maneuver under Kelly, who's torso was taking up most of the space in the cockpit. The ship suddenly executed a series of wild loops.

"Guys, this is too much," Kelly whined. I gotta get out of here. I'm gonna get sick."

"There's not enough room in here for you to get sick!" shouted Colin. His mind conjured the image of a slimy mess spilled across the cockpit. "Just try to hold on a little longer. One way or another this will all be over soon."

With great painful difficulty Colin squeezed under Kelly while Diane hurried to pry her way into the pilot's seat. The ship began zig zagging sharply. Colin wondered if these erratic movements were preventing the Brelac from establishing a firm target lock on the ship. With three fighters firing on their tail he did not expect to survive this long.

Colin contorted his body under Kelly in a tight fetal position. He apologized to Blair after his head and elbows accidently struck Blair's face. Diane crawled past Colin, painfully thrusting her elbow and foot onto his left arm and leg. Finally she placed herself into the pilot's seat, while leaning under Kelly's intruding body. She strapped herself in and firmly grasped the control sticks. At this moment Colin fully expected her to take charge of the situation and use her highly praised flying skills to get the scout craft to safety. Colin was confused when he watched Diane's head quickly swivel from one section of the instrument panel to another.

"Diane, anything wrong?" Colin inquired.

"No. I mean, I don't think so. I mean…my mind is a blank," Diane's incoherent response.

"Your mind is a blank?" Colin repeated in disbelief. He was beginning to wonder if he should have remained as the acting pilot.

"My mind is blank!" Diane snapped back. "I don't know what any of these things do!"

Colin stared wide eyed at Diane and could not believe what he had just heard. This was the person who's lives everyone was depending on. "Diane, I was under the impression that you were the greatest pilot in the Protectorate. If that was a joke then you should have told us back when we were on the ground."

"It wasn't a joke!" Diane roared back. "I'm the best damn pilot there is!" Diane turned back and leered menacingly at Blair. "What the hell did you people do to me?"

"You suffered brain damage when you were brought to us," Blair's explanation. "That could account for your memory loss. Don't panic. It might be temporary."

"It'll be permanent if we get shot out of space," Colin argued. "We need a competent pilot right now or we're dead."

"Try using the control sticks," Blair suggested. "Maybe everything will slowly come back to you."

Diane followed Blair's instructions. She pulled the control sticks sharply towards herself. The ship suddenly lurched upward. Diane began pressing a number of buttons and switches. She tried to read gauges that she could not understand.

"Making any progress?" Colin asked.

Diane's frustrations over her failure in handling the controls was causing her temper to ignite and boil over. "No, I'm not makin' any damn progress!" she bellowed. "You think it's easy trying to figure out how to fly this thing with you guys breathing down my neck?"

Colin was immediately insulted. "Well sorry, Forgive me for not putting up a tarp so that you can have a little privacy."

"Let's not argue now," Kelly pleaded. "Let's concentrate on getting away from those ships out there before they blast us."

"I'm working on it," was Diane's reply. She studied the controls for a moment. "I think I've got a fairly good idea of how these sticks work. With a little practice I think I can pick the asteroid we can crash into."

Colin ignored that morbid joke. Diane continued to work the various controls at her fingertips. She desperately needed to make an instant breakthrough. An unexpected result came when she pressed three buttons on the instrument panel. The ship thrust forward sharply and was swallowed into a brilliant burst of white light.

CHAPTER 17

▼

Inside the scout ship the occupants were completely in the dark about their destination. They could only try to endure the cramped space inside the ship's tiny cockpit and somehow try to enjoy the ride.

Blair explained this new situation that the ship was thrust into. "We've made a jump into hyperspace. We're safe."

Peering out through the window Colin and the others could see nothing except the swirling blue and white lights of hyper-dimensional space.

"Any idea where we're going?" Colin asked.

"No idea," Blair replied. "Chances are the ship is heading for a set of pre-programmed coordinates. All we can do is wait until we arrive. Where ever we arrive."

Colin hoped that the wait would not be long. His legs were starting to get numb. But at least his mind was at ease now. The ship had escaped destruction at the hand of the Brelac.

For the time being he and the others were safe.

The ship raced through hyperspace for an hour before the blackness of normal space returned to the window. They were totally ignorant about their new location. The ship's speed had decreased once it emerged from hyperspace but it was still racing out of control. Diane's mastery over the ship's controls was still unstable. Once the ship arrived at it's destination her biggest problem would be figuring out how to land the ship safely.

"Any idea where we are?" Diane asked Colin.

"I'm pretty sure that we're in the middle of nowhere," fumed Colin. As if he had the answer to such a stupid question. After all, Diane was the pilot. "Take a big sheet of blank paper and put a dot in the middle. That's us."

Kelly's torso squirmed. His shifting weight was bearing down on Colin's head. "Is it too much to hope that there's a bathroom aboard this thing?" Kelly inquired.

"You'd better hold that thought," Diane said. "I see something ahead."

Looking past Kelly's shoulder Colin saw a tiny blue orb suspended out in space. As the seconds passed the orb steadily grew larger, but it's true form was still vague.

"That could be a planet," Blair stated.

"There's your bathroom," Diane told Kelly.

An unknown world might be waiting for them. At the speed the ship was traveling they would not have long to greet it. As the ship neared the orb it's image rapidly grew larger. "Diane, we're heading for that thing awfully fast," said Colin. 'Is there any way you can stop before we have a disaster?"

"I'll just throw an anchor out of the window and maybe we'll snag onto a rock," was her sarcastic reply.

"This is no time for jokes!" Colin scolded her. "I want to know if we can walk out of this thing alive after you make a landing."

"I'll try my best. But I can't promise that we won't be spread out across this planet when we hit."

Diane's best would have to be good enough. She held a firm grip on the control sticks and attempted to guide the ship in slowly.

Without warning a large shining object streaked past the ship's window. It startled Diane so much that she screamed and let go of the control sticks. The ship titled sharply to the left. Diane grabbed the control sticks before the ship turned upside down.

The object appeared again. A silvery blur flashing in front of the ship. The sight of it alarmed Colin. "What was that?"

The object flew in front of the ship a third time. Now at a reduced speed. They were now able to get a better look at it. It was a spacecraft. Colin could not identify it's silvery boomerang shaped form as being either a Protectorate or Brelac craft.

Another ship appeared. This one was flying on a swift collision course with the scout craft. Just as it appeared that both ships would crash into each other the alien ship veered upward and flew out of sight. Another ship flew across the window, coming so close that Diane swerved the scout ship to the left to try and miss it. It was obvious that there were more than just one identified ship out there. And they were flying rings around the scout ship. Watching their daring maneuvers was highly unnerving.

"They're coming at us awfully fast, Diane,"Colin warned. "Can't you do something?"

"I'll throw out a couple of speed bumps! Think that will slow them down?" she lashed back.

A message came in over the ship's radio. It was a female voice sounding humorless and firm. "This is Panther Squadron Leader, Dayson to scout craft. Please give the required identification and security code."

"Panther Squadron?" said Diane. A broad smile beamed across her face. "Those are Protectorate ships. We're saved."

The voice on the radio repeated the request. "This is Panther Squadron Leader, Dayson to scout craft. Please give the required identification and security code. If not then we'll be forced to take the appropriate action against you."

"Appropriate action?" asked Diane.

Blair knew what that meant. "They're going to blast us out of space," he exclaimed. "Give them some identification."

Diane nervously pressed the button on the instrument panel to activate the transmitter. She began to recite an apprehensive message to Dayson. "My name is Captain Diane Christy. I have black hair...I...well. I'm about six feet tall. I'm twenty four. I was born on March third—"

Colin cut her off quickly. "Diane, try not to make it too personal," he snapped. "Just tell them who we are."

At Colin's suggestion Diane used a different approach to her address. "This is Captain Diane Christy of Silencers Squad," she said into the radio.

For a minute there was silence. Colin feared that the ships would start firing. Then came a response.

"Silencers? Never heard of you."

"We're a newly formed squad," Diane explained.

"What are you doing out here?"

"We were running from the Brelac. They just invaded Nocturne."

"We weren't alerted about Nocturne being invaded," Dayson informed Diane. "Assuming that it has been."

"I can't give you any video clips as proof," Diane sharply rebuffed. "You'll just have to take my word for it."

"So you hopped into this ship and decided to head for Lodestar for safety. Without any proper identification and security code to make your approach."

"Lodestar?" Blair gasped in surprise. "We're finally going to make it to starbase Lodestar."

"If they don't shoot us at the doorstep." Colin's grim comment.

Diane continued her losing argument with Dayson. "We were in a desperate situation. My friends and I snatched the first ship we could find. We didn't know we would end up here."

What little credibility that Diane had established with Dayson was beginning to evaporate. "Do you expect me to believe any of this, lady? Assuming that you really are a lady."

Kelly heard that remark. He could not resist adding in a comment of his own. "She's no lady."

Dayson issued a stern warning. "I'm going to give you the benefit of the doubt. I'll allow you to turn back or we will open fire and destroy you."

Diane finally decided to turn this argument over to Colin. "This is getting me nowhere. You'd better talk to this idiot."

Colin hoped that he would have better luck in dealing with Dayson. He spoke out in a loud crisp voice."Look, My name is Sergeant Colin McKenzie. My friends and I were just barely able to escape the Brelac forces when they invaded Nocturne. I realize that you have to maintain your security measures. But I can assure you that this is not some Brelac trick. We're on your side and we really need to land."

"Sorry Sarge. Your word carries as much weight as your friend's," Dayson quickly chided. "Turn your ship around or we'll have no choice but to open fire."

"Hold on. We have Doctor Blair Van Doren. He knows General Larkin. Will you at least listen to him?"

Dayson's position remained firm. "I'm not listening to anybody who does not have the proper identification and security codes. Turn that ship around now."

Colin's patience had eroded completely. It was obvious that being civil with Dayson was never going to work. "Look, pal. When the Brelac invaded Nocturne we almost got ourselves killed trying to defend it. We got our asses kicked and had to retreat. We got in this ship and evacuated like everyone else. We had a bumpy ride trying to outrun the Brelac fighters that were trying to blast us out of space. We don't have enough room in this ship because there's four of us crammed in here. Our pilot has a memory lapse and could'nt fly a kite, I've got a guy laying on top of my head, my legs are getting numb. And to make matters worse this same guy has to go to the bathroom. Would it really hurt that much to give us a break?"

Diane smiled at Colin's bold confrontation. "Way to go, Sarge. You really gave it to her."

"Don't celebrate just yet. She could give it right back and blast us into particles," Colin warned. He shouted one final plea into the radio. "Can you at least check with one of your superiors? What harm can that do?"

Colin did not expect Dayson to listen. Her answer took him by surprise.

"Stand by," Dayson replied. There was a pause.

After a tense minute there came a response. "You're in luck. The invasion of Nocturne has just been confirmed. I've been instructed to have you follow me back to base."

The group was overjoyed by this news. Colin was certain that Dayson could hear the chorus of laughter and cheers over her radio.

Dayson's boomerang shaped vessel moved in front of the scout ship. Colin was hopeful that Diane would not have any trouble following behind it. All she had to do was maintain a firm and steady grip on the control sticks and move them slowly. With any luck the ship should give them a slow and steady flight.

The group waited in silence for the next ten minutes as they followed behind Dayson's ship. Then they saw their destination appear through the ship's window. The blue orb that they saw turned out to be a tubular shaped structure of immense size. It's surface was aglow with thousands of brilliant lights. There was a space fleet composed of twenty triangular battlecruisers surrounding it defensively. A swarm of small oval shaped shuttles, triangular and boomerang shaped craft flew constantly back and forth from the larger ships to the structure that they were protecting.

"It's starbase Lodestar," said Blair. "A trip to Lodestar is where our adventure began. Now we're finally making our arrival."

As the ships drew closer to the enormous starbase it's image filled the scout craft's window. A message from Dayson came through on the scout craft's radio.

"Panther Squadron Leader, Dayson to Silencers. We are approaching landing bay six. Cut your speed and stay behind me. They have an area cleared for us to land."

Colin could see the yawning opening of the landing bay directly ahead. All Diane had to do was follow Dayson's ship inside. How hard could that be?

"Take it nice and easy," Colin advised Diane. "Just stay behind the squadron leader's ship."

Dayson's ship glided smoothly into the landing bay with the scout ship dogging close behind. Both ships flew above a wide runway with dozens of other fighters parked on both sides. They were heading for a spot that was prearranged for both ships to come to rest.

Dayson's ship reduced it's speed in order to hover and descend to a landing. The scout ship held it's current speed and course. It crashed into the rear of the fighter. Both ships hurtled down and slammed onto the runway. Their momentum caused them to skid until they reached the small flight control booth sitting at the end of the runway. The booth's two flight controllers were just barely able to burst through the doorway and escape. Both ships plowed into the frail metal booth and ripped it apart. Then they came to a halt.

Colin was covered in shards of clear plastic. The impact of the crash had shattered the window. After being rammed against the instrument panel his legs hurt worse than ever. He heard the deep toned buzz of a warning siren echo throughout the landing bay.

He looked over at Diane. She was slumped over the control sticks. He was instantly consumed by rage when he saw her move. "When I said stay close to the other ship I didn't mean this damn close!" he screamed.

"It was an accident!" Diane shouted back at him.

"No sense in arguing about it now," said Colin. The only thing that mattered now was that he and his friends were still alive. "Is everyone ok?"

"My ribs are a little sore, but I'll live," Blair responded.

"My damn head hurts," Kelly feebly whimpered. "I think I busted the window."

Diane unstrapped herself and made an assessment of her performance. "This aint' so bad. I expected this crate to shatter like an egg but it held up. Thank God I was able to bring this thing down in one piece."

Kelly held her achievement in contempt. "If I were a crash test dummy I"d have a better appreciation for your skills."

Diane became enraged by that comment. "Hey, go to hell Kirby! I'm the best damn pilot in the stinkin' Protectorate. I've got two hundred and thirty kills to prove it!"

"With all those kills you must have flown more passengers than combat missions," Kelly chided.

Colin thought that he had better defuse the tension between these two before a fight broke out. It was a frustrating chore. "Let's not waste time bickering among ourselves. We're all alive. That's what counts."

Colin shot a glance out of the broken window and saw flames dancing from the rear of Dayson's ship. "We'd better get out of here before that fire gives us a major problem."

Diane pressed the button to open the hatch. Blair crawled back, allowing Kelly to follow. After he crawled over Colin's head Colin now had room to rise and move out of the cockpit. Colin took another look at the fire and became greatly concerned about the damage that the crash had caused. "They're not going to be happy about the mess that we made here."

Diane displayed little concern about the consequences. "I already told you it was an accident. The ship just went out of control. What are they gonna do? Slap a fine on me?"

Diane and Colin emerged from the ship to be greeted by dozens of troopers aiming guns in their direction. The frowns on their faces indicated that they were unhappy about the damage to their landing bay. Their retaliation would be more than a mere fine.

A hatch on top of the crashed fighter opened with a loud hydraulic hiss. A young black female pilot, Panther Squadron Leader Dayson climbed out of her ship and jumped onto the runway. She drew her laser pistol from her belt and headed towards the scout ship's occupants. She shoved her way through the mob and raised her gun.

Dayson looked over the startled group. "Which one of you idiots is the pilot of this piece of crap?"

Kelly and Blair both pointed at Diane. Diane raised her hand. "I am. Captain Diane Christy," she confessed with pride.

"Then you die first,"Dayson hissed. She aimed her pistol at Diane's head.

CHAPTER 18

▼

Doctor Fenlow was in the Viperhawk's control room watching the telepathic images that Succubus was providing. He observed waves of Protectorate troopers in full retreat as the Viperhawk assaulted Dragos, the last Protectorate base on Trillion. Fenlow was in good spirits because the Viperhawk was functioning as perfectly as planned. Dozens of fighter squadrons were sent out to engage the Viperhawk, but it's power overwhelmed them easily.

It's multiple gun turrets, powered by pure psionic energy generated by Succubus, destroyed the fighters in waves.

Fenlow considered the attack against the Viperhawk to be a feeble waste of effort. Succubus also generated an impenetrable shield of psionic force that easily deflected the enemy firepower. While the shielding's stability appeared to be a success Fenlow was hoping to test it against a greater threat than a swarm of paltry fighters.

Fenlow was disappointed to learn that the Reploids had somehow escaped from Nocturne. A quick scan by Succubus revealed no traces of Colin, Diane or Kelly on the entire planet. No matter, Fenlow's opinion. He shrugged off his failure to locate the Reploids. He was already executing a contingency plan to acquire them. As for Nocturne, he ordered Succubus to obliterate the base completely. After which, he diverted the Viperhawk to other bases in different sectors. With Succubus' telepathic scanning it was an easy task for the computer to locate every Protectorate base on the planet. Just as easy as it would be to destroy them.

This was the fifth base that the Viperhawk had attacked. After this one fell the entire planet would be under the complete control of the Brelac. Fenlow arrived at each base before his Brelac allies. They would arrive just in time to find a deep smoking crater burned into the ground. Only a handful of fleeing troopers would remain for them to mop up.

Succubus projected the image of six fighters approaching for another attack. Their laser cannons blazing away but were unable to penetrate the Viperhawk's shields. Succubus dealt with them automatically. The Viperhawk's laser turrets targeted and destroyed all six ships in a rapid succession.

Now Fenlow observed several laser cannons and rectangular missile turrets rising from their protective underground housings around the perimeter of the base. Fenlow dismissed the possibility of these weapons posing any viable threat to the ship. He would allow them to pelt the Viperhawk's shields, granting them the dignity of fighting back.

"Succubus, fire at will," Fenlow's order.

The crystal assembly that was installed at the ship's nose glowed red with an arcane power. This was the focal point for the discharge of the Viperhawk's main weapon. Succubus provided Fenlow with a perfect view as the assault took place. He watched as the ship discharged a flaming torrent of devastating energy down on Dragos. In an instant Dragos' airfield, buildings, hovertanks and personnel were enveloped in an enormous explosion and an expanding mushroom cloud of flame that reached into the sky. Dragos was totally obliterated. There would be no recognizable structures remaining. No occupants would survive. This was another successful display of the Viperhawk's power. Fenlow was greatly pleased.

The deep voice of Succubus made an unexpected announcement. "There is an incoming message from Major Clive Danton."

"Send it through," said Fenlow.

Danton's scowling face appeared below the image of the carnage outside. He was transmitting from his personal shuttle craft. "Is this becoming a habit with you?" he growled in displeasure. "I was hoping to find any useful data or prisoners down there. Now there's not even so much as a paved spot for me to land. Just like all the others."

"You should be grateful that I've saved you the trouble," Fenlow replied with a smile. "There was really nothing down there of any value. And besides, with this last base gone we now control the entire planet. Now perhaps after this little display of power the government will jump at the chance to call for an immediate cease fire."

Succubus made another announcement. "There is a message coming in from The Brelac Supreme Commander, Bane Mariner."

Fenlow was in no mood to speak to Mariner now. But he thought that it would be wise to at least hear what his benefactor wanted. "Send it through," Fenlow ordered in a dry voice.

Next to Danton's image Fenlow was greeted by Mariner's toothy grinning face. "Greetings Doctor. I just had to call when I heard the news. Major Danton informed me that you've got this Viperhawk up and running. And that you're making a big impression on Trillion."

Fenlow gazed at the towering billows of fire and black smoke that rose from the deep and expansive crater that was once Dragos. "Yes sir. A very big impression."

"Sounds good. I can't wait to personally see what this ship of yours can do."

"You won't be disappointed," replied Fenlow.

"I hope not," Mariner returned. "General Lagar and I will be arriving to join you in another hour."

Fenlow was not enthusiastic about having to entertain guests at such a crucial time. But then he concluded that Mariner's presence would prove to be highly useful to the next phase of his plans. He put on a cordial face. "Then we'll see you soon," said Fenlow. Mariner's image blinked out.

Fenlow addressed Major Danton. "If you have any concerns then you'll have to save them until later, Major. I have preparations to make."

"Preparations?" Danton barked in irritation. "Preparations for what?"

"To end this war within the next few hours."

CHAPTER 19

▼

Colin sat on his cot in the large cell that he and his friends were confined in. In his opinion there was nothing more humiliating that being arrested and jailed by your own military-twice. In spite of his anger Colin was thankful that the troopers in the airbay restrained themselves from using physical violence against he and his friends. Instead they were brought to this cell and held here until further notice.

Kelly and Diane were laying quietly on their cots. Blair was slowly walking about the cell for the tenth time. Colin had been in this room for so long that he had lost all track of time. But while the group was here they were putting that time to good use. Blair was working with them to expand the use of their powers. He had Colin and Kelly practice using their abilities until they were becoming more versatile. Kelly discovered that he could alter his psionic energy to mimic other forms such as light and sound. Kelly also learned how to alter his psionic shield to either absorb or reflect energy. Although he stated that he was not too eager to test the durability of either shield under enemy fire.

Colin's control over his electrical based power also widened. He could exercise a form of mental control over most electrically conductive materials. That fully explained his ground splitting trick back on Trillion. Colin hoped that he now had full control over this powerful ability.

Everyone came to attention when the door suddenly slid open. A Captain stepped inside. He firmly delivered orders with a grim face. "Look alive. You're all to come with me."

No one bothered to ask where the Captain would take them. After being confined in the room for so long Colin felt grateful for a chance to leave. The wide corridors of Lodestar were bustling with activity. There seemed to be hundreds of troopers moving about with haste. Passing troopers stopped to raise their hands to salute the Captain.

The Captain brought the group to a busy landing bay. Pilots and crews were scrambling to reach their ships. Colin decided that it was time to get some answers from their mysterious escort. "Do you mind if I ask what's going on here?"

Colin noticed that the Captain seemed to be nervous. He stopped and quickly scanned the area. "I'm Captain Robert Burns, Special Operations. You're all to accompany me on a highly important mission."

"What kind of a mission?" Colin inquired.

"A first strike," replied Burns. "Right now we're assembling our forces to make a major offensive against the Brelac. Our goal is to silence Fenlow by any means. We don't have much time. We'd better board our ship and depart. We have to reach our objective while the Brelac's security is still low."

Burns took them over to an unoccupied corner. The personnel in the landing bay saluted Burns and went on with their own activities. No one stopped to question this odd group sulking about.

At the mention of a ship Diane rushed beside Burns and immediately took charge. "If we're getting a new ship then we need one that has lots of leg room. Especially leg room up front. Our last ship was too cramped. And softer seats. The pilot's seat in that little scout ship was too damn hard. And don't forget head room."

Colin could almost laugh at the inane demands that Diane was making. "Do you want a ship or do you want to drive a sedan into battle?"

They approached a spacecraft that could possibly satisfy Diane. They marveled at it's design. It's long golden hulled form was twice the size of the scout ship that they arrived in. Unlike their scout ship this vessel was fully armed for combat. The two small wings on the side of the ship were actually housings for twin laser cannons and a small stock of missiles. At the rear section were two broad wings. Bulb shaped gun turrets with twin laser cannons were mounted on their tips. On the top of the ship was a dome shaped gun turret with twin laser cannons. Beneath the ship was an open ramp waiting to admit it's new occupants.

"We're taking Corvette," Burns said. "It's a new variation on our assault cruiser. What do you think of her?"

Diane revealed her feelings quickly. "I like it. We can do a lot of serious damage with a ship like this."

"Especially after we crash it," Kelly's comment. Clearly the memory of the previous crash was still fresh in his mind.

"Let's get moving. We've got a battle to win," Burns said with authority.

Colin and Diane lead the way up the ramp and into the ship. Burns was keeping a close watch over the activities in the landing bay while Kelly and Blair boarded next. After traveling in the tiny scout ship Colin was thankful that Corvette had larger accommodations. There was a spacious passenger compartment that could hold a platoon of troopers. Colin followed Diane inside the cockpit. There would be plenty of space to sit and move in here. There were two seats Diane took her place in the pilot's seat. Colin sat down next to her.

Burns entered the cockpit. There was an annoyed grimace on his face when he saw Diane sitting in the pilot's seat. "What are you doing?" he impatiently asked Diane.

"I'm flying us outta here," she replied. Not bothering to look at Burns. She was carefully examining the large control panel in front of her. This assault cruiser had twice the buttons and gauges that the scout possessed. A few of which were not labeled. Without the proper training their functions could only be guessed at.

Colin was humbled by this technology. "This looks complicated."

"A jigsaw puzzle with missing pieces is complicated," Diane jeered back. "This is a pain in the ass."

"Flying Corvette is a job for a skilled pilot," Burns told Diane.

"That's me," Diane returned. She was adamant on her position. "Captain Diane Christy. I've got two hundred and thirty confirmed kills under my belt." Diane's eyes were still going over the many buttons and switches on the panel. "Which one of these starts the engines?"

Colin spoke in Diane's defense. "Diane is really a great pilot. She's just been out of action for a while and needs to get reacquainted with the controls. Perhaps you can help her?"

It was certain that Diane was not going to move from that seat. And Burns seemed to be too agitated to fight with her. He kept looking out of the window as if he were expecting someone. He exhaled a long sigh of frustration.

"Ok, Ace. lets make this brief," Burns calmly stated. "There's a button marked power generator at the right side of the control sticks. Press it."

Diane pressed the button. A powerful vibration surged through the entire ship as it's cold fusion generator came to life. There was a loud beep. Then a small monitor above the control sticks was activated. The statement, 12:00 A.M. was flashing.

"I don't think that's the right time," Diane told Burns.

"Don't worry about that. You can set it later," said Burns. "Now go to that little panel on the left side of the control sticks. This will activate the ship's engines. There are six buttons. The two top buttons are for your main engines. The two in the middle are for your primary thrusters. The ones on the bottom are for your secondary thrusters."

Diane pressed all six buttons.

"To reduce main engine power and kick in your thrusters for take off and landings press the first switch on the side of the left control stick."

Burns reached over and pressed a series of buttons on the panel. Four numbers appeared on a small monitor above them.

I've entered the coordinates into the hyperspace controls. Just pull back on the left control stick to lift us off. Then kick in the main engines and we're on our way."

Diane pulled the control stick back slowly. Colin strapped himself into his seat when he saw that the ship was rising into the air. Then Diane slowly pushed both sticks forward. The ship tilted from side to side as it flew down the runway and headed for the opening. To Colin's great relief the ship entered space without any unfortunate incident. Burns reached for the control panel and pressed a button. The ship's speed increased. Then he pressed a button on the hyperspace controls. Corvette was swallowed by the bright white flash of a forced wornhole. Off to it's new destination.

CHAPTER 20

▼

General Larkin hurried to reach landing bay six. He arrived at Lodestar a few hours ago. He was in the central command center trying to organize a full scale offensive against the Brelac's powerful new warship. He was informed about the loss of assault cruiser, Corvette. And who had taken it. It was a most unusual report. Once he reached the landing bay he headed straight for the flight control booth. There was a trooper standing by waiting for him. He snapped to attention and gave a salute when Larkin approached.

"At ease," Larkin told him. "Tell me what happened."

The trooper gave his account of what happened. "Two hours ago assault cruiser, Corvette launched without authorization. And without it's assigned crew. Then it made a warp jump and escaped before our fighter patrols could intercept it."

"And now they could be anywhere," Larkin added. "And it's occupants?"

"Several witnesses have reported seeing a group calling themselves Silencers Squad in the landing bay. Apparently they boarded the ship and took off."

"Obviously," Larkin said quietly. He was not aware that Silencers Squad was here at Lodestar until now. He was eager to learn why they would want to steal a ship and escape. No one here posed a threat to them. "Any idea how they could have gotten out of confinement? And so quietly at that?" With the Reploid's powers a violent escape could have been easy.

"I questioned the troopers who were guarding the cell where Silencers were being held. They both stated that a Captain Robert Burns gave them a written order from you, releasing the prisoners into his custody. It had the proper clearance code."

Larkin signed no such order. "This Captain Burns obviously forged my signature and gained access to my official clearance code. No one is going to bother stopping an officer with a signed order from a high ranking General. But now the question remains. Where did they go?"

The trooper offered a theory. "Perhaps they went back to the Brelac. Maybe they were here to gather information about Lodestar's strength and our current location."

"That's insane," Larkin scoffed. When he first met the Reploids he felt that they were completely loyal. But then he remembered that they were originally Created by the Brelac. He had no idea how mentally stable they were. Larkin hated to think the worst but this was a full scale war. He had to maintain security at all costs.

"No sense in trying to trace this Captain Burns. Chances are the man is just a shadow," Larkin explained.

Larkin gazed out at the stars beyond the landing bay. He wondered if Silencers Squad could really have been spies. Could they really have reported vital information about Lodestar back to the Brelac? Whether it was true or not Larkin could not stop what was already set into motion. In another four hours the fleet of ships that he summoned from the other sectors would assemble here. Then they would embark on their mission, to hunt down the Brelac's new super warship and destroy it before it carried out the latest threat that Doctor Fenlow had recently transmitted. The capital city of Navarone on Maseklos Prime would be destroyed unless the United Protectorate surrendered immediately.

If there was a chance that the Brelac knew that they were coming then Larkin thought that it would be wise to throw them a curve. "Inform the personnel in the command center that I'm moving our timetable ahead. Instead of waiting for our reinforcements to arrive we're going to launch the defense force of battle-cruisers and fighters that are guarding Lodestar. The reinforcements will serve as replacements and remain here. We launch within the hour."

CHAPTER 21

▼

Colin was glad to see the stars of normal space returning to view. The ship had warped to it's destination. Now Colin began to worry about the mission that he and his friends were on.

"What exactly are we going to do when we reach our target?" Colin asked Burns.

"We're going to infiltrate our target from within and make a surprise attack," explained Burns. "I'll show you how we're going to do it. Diane, activate the autopilot and let me have the controls so that I can take us in."

Diane pressed a button on the control panel that Burns showed her earlier. With the automatic pilot activated Diane could safely leave the controls without the ship falling into a wild spin.

With Burns' skilled hands at the controls the ship quickly arrived at it's destination. Colin and Diane saw that they were approaching a large oval shaped spacecraft with swept forward wings. A ship that appeared to be dangerously familiar in Colin's opinion.

"There's our target," Burns announced. He guided Corvette in smoothly, then stopped it next to the target ship. He then pressed two buttons on the control panel. "Extending docking tube."

Corvette was mildly shaken by the impact of the two ships connecting with a mild boom.

"Here we are," Burns said. He rose from his seat. "We're infiltrating this enemy ship."

Colin was curious about the ease in which Corvette had penetrated into enemy space without encountering any defenses. "Strange how we didn't run into any fighters. Maybe the Brelac are allowing us to get this close so that they can spring a trap."

Burns explained, "We slipped through a hole in their defenses. But we only have a limited time to act."

Burns lead the group behind the passengers section. The airlock door was on the left side of the bulkhead. "Prepare yourselves," he warned.

Burns pressed a button on the wall panel to open the door. The airlock door slid open to reveal those three robotic creatures waiting on the other side. The same creatures that nearly killed Colin, Diane and Kelly back on Trillion.

Burns produced a laser pistol from his pocket and jammed it into the side of Colin's head. "Nobody moves or McKenzie dies!" he shouted.

The robots stepped forward. The group was totally helpless against these machines back on Trillion. They were just as helpless now.

"What the hell is this?" Colin demanded.

"You said it yourself." Burns smugly replied. "It's a trap."

CHAPTER 22

▼

Major Danton noticed that Fenlow was completely calm as he stood in front of the Viperhawk's airlock door. They were both awaiting the arrival of two highly important visitors. Mariner and General Lagar. Any moment their ship was due to arrive and dock with the Viperhawk. For that reason Danton had an entire nest of butterflies swarming inside his stomach. A visit from your two highest ranking superiors will always be just cause to restrain an urge to fly into a blind panic.

Danton suddenly heard the thundering boom of a docking tube connecting with the airlock. It was evident that Mariner's personal cruiser had arrived. Danton's heart fluttered. He wished that he had more time to prepare for this visit. There was the sound of compressed air being flushed through the docking tube. While the dark, wedge shaped vessel was docked here Mariner's escort, the Elite Guardian Squadron would flank the ship in a protective formation. The firepower of four attack carriers and six destroyers always traveled with Mariner and would battle furiously to protect him.

The airlock door slid open. Mariner's personal guard marched out of the airlock first. Ten soldiers with their rifles in hand. Then Mariner and Lagar strode out of the airlock. The soldiers lined up along the corridor and snapped to attention as their superiors passed by. Danton greeted them with a quick salute.

Fenlow smiled, rushing over to Mariner and Lagar to shake their scaley hands. "Welcome to the Viperhawk. I promise that you will both have a unique experience here."

"Coming all this way I hope so," said Mariner. "Am I to understand that you've conquered Trillion single handed?"

"Precisely," Fenlow returned with a proud smile. "Save for a few weakly armed stragglers all major opposition on the planet has been removed. Quickly and effectively, thanks to the superiority of psionically powered weaponry."

"It's a shame that you didn't wait until Lagar and I arrived," Mariner replied. "I was eager to see what this psionically powered weaponry of yours can do.

"You'll get your chance," Fenlow assured him. "You and your squadron will accompany us to our next target. Maseklos Prime."

Lagar was immediately apprehensive about Fenlow's plan. "Eleven ships attacking the heart of the Protectorate?" Only a full scale assault by a full armada would be able to break through their defenses."

"A feat that would take you months," Fenlow rebutted. "Trust me. We have more than sufficient power to do the job. You will see the power of this new weapon's technology in action to end the war."

Mariner hesitated before answering. "We'll see. I'm putting a lot of faith in you, Fenlow. For the hope of our survival I hope that you are right. But in the meantime We'd like a tour of this ship. Let's start with this wonder computer of yours."

"Succubus," replied Fenlow. Major Danton will take you to the control center to have a look. While that's happening I have a few personal matters to attend to. I'll get back to you as soon as I can."

Without another word Fenlow turned and walked away.

"Your pal, Fenlow seems to be a little over enthused about his creation," Mariner told Danton.

"He has a good reason, sir. This ship wields awesome firepower. Conquering Trillion single handedly is an impressive accomplishment," Danton said in Fenlow's defense. "The ships is easy to control. It's main computer, Succubus, follows verbal commands. I've accessed it several times."

"Then I assume that you can take control and manage things without Fenlow," Mariner stated.

Danton nodded. "Yes sir."

"Good. Then we'll have no further reason to keep Fenlow alive. We already have everything we need from him. He's already shown us his advanced in-vitro cloning process. Back at Rantraven we've set up an experimental program to create a few cloned soldiers in record time. If it works then we'll begin full scale production and crank out an army of unstoppable troops practically overnight."

Lagar added, "Each one will be given Fenlow's psionic enhancements. And programmed to be as ruthless in battle as rabid dogs. But also as loyal as sons.

We'll also need to construct more ships like this Viperhawk. But I still would like to see this thing in action. That will give me the chance to see if it's worth it."

"You won't be disappointed, sir," Danton assured him.

A soldier from Mariner's cruiser came charging through the airlock. He was gasping excitedly. "Sir, there's an urgent subspace message for you. It's from the research section at Rantraven. There's been an accident."

Mariner and Lagar bolted through the airlock. Danton followed closed behind them. If this accident was serious enough that the scientists at Rantraven had to contact Mariner personally then Danton feared the worst. The cruiser's bridge was only a short distance down the dimly lit corridor. They charged into the small bridge. There were only four crewmen sitting at their assigned consoles. Mariner headed straight for the communications console.

"Mariner here. What's going on?"

A frantic voice responded. "This is Captain Armatige. We were working on the advanced cloning system when our computers suddenly erased all our data. Then there was an explosion. Seven technicians were killed. One of them was Major Dunnager, the head of the project."

"What was erased?" asked Mariner.

"All the project data. The formula for Fenlow's nutrient fluid, his mental programming process, his psionic implant designs. Even his designs for the Cybernoids. The computers just summoned up all the data and erased it."

"All of it?" Danton gasped. This was the worst disaster that he could imaging. The news of the explosion became insignificant.

"Can anything be salvaged?" Mariner desperately asked.

"Nothing is left, sir. I'm sorry."

"Didn't anybody think to get anything down on paper?" Mariner bellowed. "Do you have any idea how valuable that data was?"

"Paper?"

"Never mind, idiot! What about the explosion?"

"It was a very powerful blast. Obviously from an explosive device of some sort. We have no idea who could have planted it. The entire lab and the cloning project are a total loss."

Mariner screamed aloud in a rage and slammed his fist down onto the communications console. "I want you to find the son of a bitch who set off that blast! A Human couldn't possibly breach our security, so it has to be one of our own! Find him!"

Danton pondered Mariner's words. No Human could possibly penetrate Rantraven base. Not unless he was given a free reign to do so. Such as Doctor Howard Fenlow.

Mariner turned to Lagar and Danton. "Well, gentlemen. It would seem that we'll still have a need for our good Doctor Fenlow after all."

CHAPTER 23

▼

Colin sat against the wall of this small room, still feeling like a complete idiot for allowing he and his friends to walk into the trap that Captain Burns and those robotic creatures had prepared for them. The others were also forced to sit against the wall. Colin brooded over the fact that their captors could have provided a containment cell with at least one small cot or a chair. Sitting on this cold, hard floor was very uncomfortable.

"I wonder what's going to happen to us next?" said Blair. "It certainly seems that whoever is behind this went through a lot of trouble to get this group into their clutches."

"You can bet that we aint' here to sign autographs," Diane stated. "Chances are that they want information. And the way I see it they can only get it by putting us under a brain scan and sucking our minds out a little bit at a time."

Blair recoiled at Diane's morbid description of their possible fate.

"Nobody's going to do any sucking," Colin firmly declared. "We'll find a way to get out of this mess."

"Do you think those robots are still outside?" Kelly fearfully asked.

"You can bet on it," replied Colin. "And why not? They're the perfect guards. They beat us pretty easily back on Trillion. And we don't really know how many there are. For all we know there could be a few dozen of them manning this ship."

The image of a man in a white lab coat suddenly appeared in front of the door. His sudden appearance startled everyone. He addressed them in a booming voice. "You have nothing to fear from my Cybernoids. That is, as long as you cooperate with me."

Colin was wondering how long it would take for one of their captors to greet them. He rose up and fearlessly confronted the apparition while the others jumped to their feet and backed away in fear.

"Cybernoids?" So that's what they're called. And who are you?" Colin boldly inquired.

"It's a pity that Doctor Trevor didn't program you to recognize me as your creator. Doctor Howard Fenlow."

The word, creator instantly caught Colin's attention.

Blair moved in closer. "Doctor Fenlow? Is that really you?"

Fenlow smiled. "In a way. You're being addressed by a telepathic projection transmitted by my computer, Succubus. Succubus is the main power behind this ship. I trust that you are all feeling well. I'd like to officially welcome you aboard the Viperhawk. I apologize for the deception but it was necessary to bring you here. I originally planned to have you Reploids destroyed back on Trillion. But when I learned that you narrowly escaped with your lives I decided to alter my plans for you. Instead of killing you I had you all brought here alive."

"You had us brought here?" asked Blair. "For what purpose? To defect like you and Captain Burns did?"

Fenlow laughed briefly. "I'm sorry, but the being that aided your escape from Lodestar was not a real Protectorate officer. Captain Burns is a Reploid agent. I had him infiltrate Nocturne during the attack. That way I could have a waiting agent within the military. Then you Reploids escaped from my Cybernoids. That gave me the chance to put Burns to use. I needed someone to gain your trust and bring you here peacefully."

Colin hated to be reminded that he and his friends were easily duped into this trap. "Now that you have us here what do you want?"

"I consider the Viperhawk to be the greatest creation of my career. It's power will end this insane war and start a new era for our people. I'd like for you, Blair, one of my most trusted assistants. And my creations, The Reploids to be a part of that era. I want you all to share my triumph and join me."

Colin saw no incentive in Fenlow's offer. "That also means joining the Brelac like you did. That's not a savory idea."

"Working with the Brelac was necessary," said Fenlow. "I needed their resources. And their presence is crucial to the success of my plan. I'm going to need them to help me to expand the Protectorate. Bigger and better than before. Everyone will benefit from this. Even the Brelac. Will you join me?"

Colin looked back at, Blair, Diane and Kelly. There was a pause of silence between them. He gave his answer back to Fenlow. "We're not interested. When we enlisted in the military we took an oath to guard the Protectorate and it's citizens from all danger to life and limb. We don't take that oath lightly. Maybe you shouldn't either."

"So it appears that Colin McKenzie is speaking for the entire group," said Fenlow. "You seem to be adamant on your position. That's unfortunate. But I suppose that it's my fault. I should have instructed Doctor Trevor to program you all to be more loyal to your creator. Then having you join me would not be such a problem. But in spite of this I can remain benevolent. I'll give you one hour to consider my offer. Agree to work with me and you can all walk out of this room. It not, then my Cybernoids will insure that none of you will leave here alive."

Fenlow's image blinked out, leaving the group with a serious dilemma. Either join with an admitted defector or die. In Colin's mind there was no real choice. He could not voluntarily join Fenlow and the Brelac. He hoped that Diane and Kelly felt the same way. As for Blair, Colin now had several vital questions in his mind. It was possible that only Fenlow or Blair could provide him with the answers.

"Creator? Programs? What was he talking about?" Colin inquired of Blair.

Diane and Kelly both advanced towards Blair and flanked him closely. Blair looked down at the floor and exhaled a deep breath. "Guys, I've got a lot of explaining to do."

CHAPTER 24

▼

Mariner was highly impressed as he studied Fenlow's computer, Succubus. He had never encountered such an advanced technology of this type before. He was thinking that it would be fascinating to have full access to Succubus and find out exactly what it could do. But as he explained to Lagar there would be plenty of time to explore the computer later. For now he would just settle for replacing the valuable data that he needed.

Mariner noticed that Succubus was studying him in return. The image of a gaping eye followed his every move. It alarmed him at first. Then Danton assured him that it was merely a harmless telepathic projection. Another reason to marvel at this machine of Fenlow's.

Fenlow entered the room.

"This is quite a piece of hardware you've got here, Doctor," said Mariner. "I can just imagine what it can do."

"I doubt that," Fenlow replied in a dull voice.

Mariner shrugged off that blatant insult to his intelligence. "But still, you have to admit that this is a remarkable piece of work. A fully functioning cybernetic computer system. Part machine, part living tissue. Managing every function of this ship. And able to generate enough power to take out a Protectorate military base in a single blow. When you first described this project to me I had my doubts. Now here it is."

Fenlow had no comments.

Mariner continued. "This goes beyond anything my scientists could come up with. I have to hand it to you, Fenlow. You're a true genius. Which brings me to the point. I've received a report about an unfortunate incident back at Rantraven.

There was an explosion in the lab where we were setting up an experimental rapid cloning facility. The whole damn thing was a total loss."

Fenlow was unruffled by the incident. "That's old news. And I should know. I caused it."

Mariner found that hard to believe. "You?"

"Of course. I sent one of my Reploids to do the job," Fenlow calmly replied.

"How?" asked a doubtful Mariner.

"Very easy. I've established a small network of Human and Brelac Reploids, infiltrating both ranks. The Reploid that I sent to Rantraven easily blended in with your scientists, planted the bomb, and left to await further orders."

Mariner was speechless. He had no idea that Fenlow could accomplish such feats. Especially with Danton here. "Danton, how is all this possible?"

"Don't waste your time asking him," Fenlow stated. "I did everything under his nose. Just like I purged all traces of my data from your computers."

"You're saying that you're responsible for that too? How?"

"Don't be so dense," said Fenlow. "You're standing in the room with my greatest instrument. Succubus. The most advanced computer, and the most powerful psychic mind ever created. It was easy for it to penetrate your computer systems at Rantraven through a subspace uplink. It deleted all traces of my data just as easily as it monitored your every move. As well as your intentions to eliminate me."

"Eliminate you?" Mariner tried to maintain a cloak of innocence. "I don't know what you're talking about."

"Don't insult my intelligence," Fenlow bit back. "Succubus informed me that you planned to have me eliminated just as soon as the Viperhawk was completed. It pays to be able to verbally communicate with your tools. Especially tools that can read minds."

Mariner was caught. He had to think of a halfway believable story to tell Fenlow. Then he began to wonder why he should even bother. The only reason that he kept Fenlow alive was that he was useful. Now Mariner was surrendering to the urge to do without the Human.

Mariner confessed with a toothy smile. "You got me, Doctor. Why deny it? In addition to the Viperhawk I wanted your genetic data for my own plans. And of course, I still want them."

Mariner drew his plasma pistol from his weapon's belt and aimed it at Fenlow. Following his lead Lagar and Danton drew theirs.

Fenlow was not fazed by this threat. He still held his tranquil demeanor. "Ah, guns, threats. I was wondering when you'd get around to this."

"You're a little smug for someone who's about to die," Mariner hissed. "Since you ordered this thing, Succubus to erase the data from my computers then I figure that you must have it all stored in it's memory. It's too valuable for you to loose. Give me the data or we start target practice."

"I have nothing to fear," Fenlow admitted. "After all, I'm still holding all your dreams for the future. But if it will make you feel any better."

Fenlow walked over to Succubus and pressed two keys on it's keyboard. A small tray below the keyboard slid open and revealed a three inch silvery disk. Fenlow removed the disk and handed it to Mariner.

"What the hell is this?" asked Mariner.

"The complete procedure for creating in-vitro Reploids," Fenlow calmly explained. "As well as my mental programming procedure, my psionic implant designs, my formula for the nutrient solution, and the designs for my Cybernoids and Succubus."

Mariner smiled. "You're not so damn smart after all, Fenlow. You think that giving me this disk will save your ass?"

"I'll let you know after you examine it first," Fenlow said. "Succubus, allow Major Danton to access the data on the disk."

Mariner thought that examining the disk before he killed Fenlow was a wise move. He handed the disk to Danton. Danton placed the disk back onto the tray and began pressing keys on Succubus' keyboard. The telepathic image of succubus' eye was replaced by paragraphs of numerical equations and words that were written in a non-english language that Mariner could not recognize. The equations could be easily understood if he could only read the words that explained them.

Danton pressed a key that advanced the text. There were complex diagrams of organic chemical formulas written with the same incoherent letters. It would appear that the entire disk was written in this same code.

"What the hell is this?" Danton demanded.

"The notation? It's one of the Old Earth languages that I've been studying," Fenlow proudly explained. "This language originated around what used to be the Mediterranean area. It's a very ancient language. It's called greek."

"Greek?" bellowed Mariner. "What the hell good is it? I can't read it!"

"I didn't think you could," Fenlow smugly returned. "Unless you've got a greek to english dictionary at home I don't advise you to kill anybody just yet."

Mariner became furious. He turned his anger to the one individual who could possibly solve this puzzle. He shoved Danton roughly towards the computer. "Do something! Fix this!" he shouted.

Danton's efforts were feeble. The most that he could do was to press a key that advanced the text so that he could inspect it entirely. Danton gave his assessment of the disk to Mariner. "I'm sorry sir. I'm afraid it's all greek to me."

Mariner exploded in a rage. His crusty lips folded up to bare his tightly clenched fangs. He was in the mood to kill. Anyone within reach. Danton slowly stepped away.

"I've had enough of you and your crap, Fenlow!" Mariner spat out. "Nobody makes me look stupid! Nobody!"

In the face of Mariner's rage Fenlow remained calm and held a triumphant smirk on his face. "And just what do you propose to do about it? The power that I've created here makes me immune to all petty threats. Especially yours. I'm sorry to say that you're the one who's usefulness has expired. You've provided me with the resources that I needed to bring this project to life. For that I am grateful. But now I require nothing else from you. The ultimate power can only be wielded by one individual. Not a collective body. And I am most qualified to be that individual."

"Then I guess that your double cross is only fair," returned Mariner. "I was planning to get rid of you after I got what I wanted. It's a shame that I couldn't get everything, but at least I'll still have this ship."

Fenlow disagreed. "You don't even have that. Looks like you've come up empty through all this. Too bad. Now I'll have Succubus disarm and restrain you."

Mariner sneered. "The computer? What's it gonna do? Whip us to death with it's extension cord?"

Fenlow ignored the question. "Succubus, disarm the Brelac."

Mariner, Lagar and Danton's plasma pistols were suddenly wrenched out of their hands by a strong and unseen force. Lagar and Danton's guns struck the side of Succubus and remained fixed there as though they were magnetized. The gun from Mariner's own hand flew towards Fenlow. He snatched it out of the air and pointed it at his three targets.

Fenlow grinned smugly while Mariner stood in bewilderment.

"Telekinesis," Fenlow proudly stated to Mariner. "It's simply another manifestation of Succubus' power. You have to admit that it comes in handy for situations like this. You were right when you said that you couldn't imagine all the things that Succubus could do. Succubus, execute hyperspace jump to Maseklos Prime. Order Mariner's fleet to do the same. Use his voice and image. It's time to put the final phase of my revised plan into action."

CHAPTER 25

▼

Walter Carnaby was thrilled as he entered the conference room. His mood was a sharp contrast to the grim looks on the faces of Rodger Bannister, John Steiner and a few others seated at the table. While on his way here Carnaby envisioned the memories of the countless meetings that he had in this dreary room. Now he had thoughts of the future. Thoughts of holding meetings within the hallowed walls of the presidential conference room. The United Protectorate was about to undergo a sweeping change. The current government would be the first target of this change. President Drennen and many others would soon be removed.

Carnaby noticed that the large video screen against the left wall was receiving a transmission. It projected the glowering face of John Crane, Secretary of Defense. A high ranking member of this clandestine group who kept his association with them a tight secret.

"Gentlemen, why the sour faces?" Carnaby asked, taking his seat.

From the video screen Crane spoke out first. "Some of us are sharing the same concerns about your man, Fenlow. And his part in this plan. His approach is just too damn bold. He could expose us all if he's not careful."

"And what if he does?" Carnaby asked, apathetic to the possibility of any danger. "When the plan succeeds we'll reveal ourselves as the leaders of the new empire that we've envisioned."

"And what if the plan should fail?" Crane demanded. "Undoubtably Fenlow now has the entire military agitated after he made the second ultimatum. Threatening to attack Maseklos Prime will not be taken lightly. Defenses are being bolstered. I'm not sure if he"ll have the power to prevail. What if the Viperhawk is damaged or destroyed, and Fenlow is captured?"

Carnaby scoffed at such notions. "Nonsense. The results at Trillion speak for themselves. Nothing can stand against this new psionic weapons technology."

"Perhaps," said Steiner. "But I'm still worried about brining the Brelac into this plan."

"I've already told you that the Brelac are a vital cog in our plan," Carnaby stated. "They provided the means to create this weapon under the guise of an alliance. And in turn we will have the means to control them. With the Brelac neutralized as a threat and the Protectorate under our power we will be able to finally realize our goal of establishing the new independent territories. A new United Protectorate of independent states, banning together in the presence of any common threat."

"And in reality governed by a new central power. With you at it's head," Bannister added. He gave out a laugh. "If the rank and file only knew that they were fighting to put a pretty new label on the same old can of worms."

Carnaby disagreed. "On the contrary. We're giving them a new government dedicated to expansion. The Protectorate hasn't grown in decades. We need to add new worlds into our sphere of influence."

"Before we conquer the universe let's concentrate on gaining control of our own back yard," Steiner reminded Carnaby.

Carnaby considered Steiner's advise. "Perhaps it would be realistic to take this one step at a time. If there are no objections then we can begin the final phase of Operation Broad Axe. I've already ordered our fleet of shuttles carrying our assault troops to launch for Maseklos Prime. On my command they will land and garrison themselves in Navarone."

"And what if President Drennen happens to be more stubborn than you realize?" asked Crane. "What if she refuses to surrender?"

To Carnaby the answer was simple. "Then Navarone becomes a crater. Our assault troops will land in the nearby city of Manheim. There we will establish a new capital and declare a new government."

"I still don't know about all this," Crane returned. "This plan had better work. I'll be putting my ass out in the open with the rest of you. I don't have to remind you of what will happen if this whole thing should fall through."

"Think positive," Carnaby advised. "I don't conceive any possibility of failure. Now if there are no further subjects to discuss I suggest that we board our shuttle. We'll accompany our assault troops when they arrive at Maseklos Prime. This is the day when Vendetta takes control."

CHAPTER 26

▼

There was a suspense filled wait as Colin watched Blair gather his thoughts and prepare to speak. Colin could not breathe as he waited. At last the truth about his, Diane and Kelly's lives would be revealed.

Blair started out with a sigh. "Here goes. Colin, Diane, Kelly. You guys are not who you think you are."

"Really?" Kelly asked. "Who exactly are we?"

"The three of you are actually complex computer programs created by Doctor Trevor, and placed into Reploid bodies that were rapidly grown through an in-vitro process. Your programs are patterned after the lives of real troopers."

"So, who exactly are these people?" Kelly asked in a skeptical tone.

"I have no idea. But that's not important. You three were the survivors of a shipment of Reploids that the Brelac were planning to use to infiltrate Helios. Your ship was shot down and we recovered you. We reprogrammed you to be Protectorate troopers. Your programs are quite complex. You each have your own personal identities, the ability to think independently and make your own decisions. All the qualities you need to be the perfect fighting machines."

"I'm already the perfect fighting machine," Diane stubbornly boasted, rejecting Blair's story. "I'm an ace fighter pilot with two hundred and thirty kills on my belt."

"Diane, you're not an ace pilot. You only think you are," Blair impatiently explained. "Doctor Trevor obviously failed to program you with the proper knowledge of flying. And you have to practice to gain the skill of an ace pilot. There were some instructional flight programs available. He could have converted them into his program for you. I'll never understand why he didn't."

His two partners may have refused to believe Blair's explanation, but to Colin all the facts were fitting neatly into place. "It all makes sense," he muttered in a cheerless voice.

"Don't tell me you believe all this?" Diane asked in amazement.

"It has to be the truth," Colin's subdued reply. "It explains a lot of things. How we came from those cylinders back at Scorpis. These powers of ours. Blair's explanation fills a lot of gaps in our lives."

Diane scoffed. "The only gap in your life is between your ears. I'm Captain Diane Christy. I'm a fighter pilot. I have two hundred and thirty kills on my belt."

Blair corrected her. "No, you're only an ace pilot in your own mind. But your skills are improving. You handled corvette really well."

"Yeah. And look where we ended up," Kelly chided. He turned to Colin. "If this is all true then what do we do about it?"

"What can we do?" Colin quickly snapped. "I'm still me. Sergeant Colin McKenzie. That's the only identity that I have. I admit that I'm really shocked about this. But that doesn't change the fact that I'm alive. And I'd like to keep on living. You don't expect me to commit suicide over it, do you?"

"Would you blow your brains out or press a button on the side of your head that says erase?" Diane asked.

"We'll deal with this problem later," Colin replied. "Right now we're going to concentrate on getting out of here and stopping Fenlow."

Colin turned away and examined the walls. As far as he could tell they appeared to be metallic. Or at least conductive to his electrical powers. Colin kneeled down to the floor and extended his hand. "Get ready," he warned.

Colin's hand touched the floor. Streams of energy flowed from his fingers and along the surface of the floor. Colin was attempting to use his ability to manipulate conductive matter and create an opening in the floor. He and the others would use it to jump down into the level below. This way they could slip past the Cybernoids guarding the door.

Colin concentrated on creating a small hole. Suddenly the entire floor began to splinter. Then it collapsed. Colin and his friends painfully and noisily crashed down into an empty room below. Everyone was briefly stunned by the fall. Colin looked up and saw the door above slide open. The Cybernoids were coming to investigate the disturbance.

CHAPTER 27

▼

Fenlow was startled by a sudden warning from Succubus.

"Silencers Squad have escaped from confinement."

"How?" Fenlow demanded.

"The Reploid, Colin McKenzie used his power to somehow disrupt the structural integrity of the floor to their confinement area. They are now in corridor B of level two. The Cybernoids are in pursuit."

Fenlow was beginning to regret the notion of sparing the lives of this group. "It would seem that Silencers are starting to become an annoyance. Maybe I should have killed them back on Trillion."

"Silencers?" Mariner inquired.

"An obsolete experiment," Fenlow cheerlessly explained. "Ungrateful lab rats. But they'll pose no threat to my plans. They're on this level. I'm sure that your guards will keep them at bay long enough for my Cybernoids to reach them. Then their presence will be eradicated."

"We have emerged from hyperspace. Arriving at the Maseklos star system," Succubus informed Fenlow.

"Continue on course for Maseklos Prime. Scan the system for any defensive forces," Fenlow ordered.

Fenlow expected Succubus' telepathic scanning of the star system to be swift and effective. Within seconds Succubus revealed it's findings.

"A large fleet of Protectorate warships have formed a blockade at coordinates four, one, one, two, eight. Three hundred and ninety ships."

"You don't expect to hold off that many ships?" Mariner asked in amazement. "Even with my guardian squadron to back you up you don't stand a chance."

"First off, I don't expect to hold off that many ships. I expect to destroy them," Fenlow calmly stated. "Second, I don't need your squadron to help me deal with anyone. Instead, I think that it's time that I've dealt with you Brelac before I deal with the Protectorate. Succubus, activate jamming sequence for type one psionic implant."

"Initiating sequence," Succubus said in compliance.

With the command uttered Fenlow's three Brelac captives cried out in pain, grasping their heads. Then their heads swivelled about as if scanning the area for something that was no longer present.

"What the hell's going on? I can't see!" Mariner squawked. His hand clawing the air for something to touch.

Fenlow explained with pride, "Succubus is jamming the interaction between your psionic implants and your nervous systems. In effect, rendering you what you were born to be. Totally blind."

Mariner snarled furiously. He lunged forward, swiping the air towards Fenlow with no hope of actually striking him.

Fenlow continued. "When you first gave me a few of your psionic implants for study I discovered a means of jamming them by projecting a stronger psionic signal along the same resonance. At the time of the discovery it's use as an effective weapon against you had a great potential. Naturally Carp and Vendetta withheld that knowledge from the military. After all, they had their own agenda. And the jamming could only be performed on a limited basis. Only a living brain could produce the needed psionic power. On a small scale at that. We needed a larger source of power with a greater means of projecting it. That's where I envisioned the concept for Succubus. A larger living generator of psionic power, enhanced by larger versions of your implants. Able to deliver a signal powerful enough to blind all Brelac within a vast range. Succubus, show me what's happening outside."

Succubus immediately displayed the chaotic image of Mariner's Elite Guardian Squadron in a state of disarray. The destroyers and attack carriers had stopped their engines. Several of the huge vessels had drifted into each other, causing major damage to their hulls. The sounds of panicked voices could be heard as the Brelac crews were desperately trying to maintain proper order aboard their ships while trying to comprehend the sudden loss of their psychic sight.

"Hear that, Mariner? Your ships are completely helpless. This takes your Elite Guardian Squadron out of the fight. Not that they were needed."

"Damn you, Fenlow! What the hell do you want?" Mariner snapped. He appeared to be ready to cede the victory to Fenlow.

Fenlow was standing secure in his new power. He was confident that no force could successfully oppose him. "I want nothing, for now. Just behave yourselves and I may find it within my heart to return your sight."

"A large fleet of Protectorate warships have emerged from hyperspace at coordinates Eight, six, one, two, eight. Two hundred vessels. They are rapidly approaching our position."

"Reinforcements," Fenlow softly muttered. "Succubus, destroy them. Then continue on course for Maseklos Prime."

CHAPTER 28

▼

Diane's hands easily ripped open the door so that she and the others could escape into the next corridor. Colin was anxious to get as far away from the Cybernoids as possible. Colin lead the group through the corridor until they came to a four way intersection. Everyone was tensely waiting to be attacked, but it seemed as though the ship were deserted. Colin knew that this was far from the truth. Their enemies were here. Probably remaining hidden while watching the group's every move. Waiting for the perfect time to strike. This gave their enemies a dangerous advantage.

"For all we know we could be walking into a trap," Colin grimly murmured."We'd better find a way to get off this ship. Maybe we can find a shuttle or some escape pods."

"I would agree with that idea under normal circumstances. But we can't leave," Blair argued. "Not until we find Fenlow. We have to try and stop him. He could destroy the Ptotectorate."

"Any idea how we can make this happen?" Kelly asked. "We're on a ship occupied by enemy forces. And those robots who thrashed us back on Trillion are right behind us."

"Then we work fast," was Colin's best answer. He was not going to delude himself. The job would be suicide. But he was compelled to try. Reploid or not he was still loyal to the Protectorate. It was his duty to try and stop Fenlow's threat to everything that he knew.

Rushing to reach the intersection the group did not expect to be greeted by Captain Burns. He emerged from the right corridor. There was a laser pistol in his hand.

"Silencers. Thank God you've escaped. I need your help. That Fenlow is a madman."

"Save it!" Colin snapped at him. "Don't insult our intelligence. We know what you really are!"

"I see that you won't be on the recall list for brains, McKenzie," Burns replied. "It's a shame that you have to be eliminated."

Ten Brelac soldiers came charging from the left corridor. They quickly raised their plasma rifles to take aim and fire. Diane let out a piercing battle cry and sprinted towards the Brelac. Blair followed her lead and bolted towards the Brelac as well. One of the Brelac managed to fire two shots that whizzed past Diane's head. Diane tackled two Brelac to the floor. Blair dove on top of one Brelac and wrestled him down. Diane quickly thrust her fist into the Brelac's head. With his skull effectively caved in the Brelac died instantly. Kelly sent streams of flaming energy from his hands that burned through the bodies of two Brelac.

Blair was able to wrench the plasma rifle from his Brelac's grasp. With a weapon in his hands he instantly spun around and gunned down two Brelac who were about to shoot at Colin. Colin responded by sending a burst of electrical energy from his fingertips that slammed one Brelac against the wall. Diane jumped up and grabbed a Brelac by his neck. She slammed his body against the wall with a crushing force that produced a moist crunch of breaking bones. Colin released more bolts that struck the two remaining Brelac. Their smoking bodies fell limply to the floor. Now the only threat that remained was Captain Burns. He retreated down the corridor and began firing back at his antagonists. His rapid movements hampered his aim. Laser bolts flew past Colin and Kelly. Diane quickly snatched up a fallen Brelac's rifle and riddled Burns with multiple plasma bolts.

Colin was relieved now that the threat of Burns and the Brelac was eliminated. "We certainly pulled that off without a hitch," he professed with amazement. The enemy was dealt with swiftly and effectively. And his squad suffered no casualties in the process. Unfortunately this weak force was not the only enemy that they had to face aboard this ship.

Colin glanced back and saw that the three Cybernoids were now storming down the corridor. Colin felt that fighting them was inevitable, but he had no desire to rush into it right this minute. He prodded the group down the right corridor, not sure of exactly where it would take them. Colin considered abandoning the goal of locating Fenlow. For now he would be grateful to stumble across a ship docked at an airlock.

There were doors on both sides of the corridor. Colin wished that he had the time to break down each one and see what was behind them. The Cybernoids chasing them would not permit it. The group approached a door at the end of the corridor. It opened by itself. Colin became suspicious. This could be a trap. But he would rather face what was in the room up ahead instead of those three deadly Cybernoids.

The group ran through the doorway and found themselves in a large circular room. In the center of the room was a tall column shaped machine. Above the machine was the image of a large eye that stared back at them. Standing next to this machine was Doctor Howard Fenlow himself. There was a pistol in his hand. He grinned triumphantly to greet them. Behind him were three Brelac. They appeared to be unarmed.

Fenlow approached the group. "It's about time you people showed up. I hope you wiped your feet before you came in here."

CHAPTER 29

▼

"Doctor Fenlow," Colin said.

"In the flesh this time," Fenlow declared, wearing a proud grin on his face.

The three Cybernoids appeared near the doorway. They were about to enter the room when Fenlow ordered them to stop. They stood guard outside the room while the door slid close.

"Don't worry about them. They won't hurt anyone," Fenlow assured the group. "Not unless I give the word. Welcome, Silencers, to the nerve center of the most powerful weapon ever conceived. Also, you have the honor of meeting my associates and benefactors. Major Clive Danton, General Owen Lagar, and the Brelac's supreme commander. Governor General Bane Mariner."

Colin looked upon Fenlow's Brelac guests with disdain. "With all the threats that you've made against the Protectorate I'm not surprised to see your Brelac masters here."

"You're obviously mistaken by the appearance here. I"m the only master in this room," Fenlow corrected. "Mariner and his two flunkies are also quite harmless. Thanks to the power that I hold over them. They're the ones who will serve me as I govern and reshape both empires. I'm already holding the Brelac in check. Now in a few moments I'll force President Drennen to surrender the United Protectorate to my authority."

"Not if we stop you first," Colin admonished. He took a step towards Fenlow and raised his hands.

An irresistibly powerful and unseen force threw Colin and the others against the wall. The impact sent a wave of pain through Colin's body. His back was pinned tightly to the wall. Kelly and Blair were equally helpless. Diane appeared to be unconscious.

"You assumed that I was just standing here helpless without my Cybernoids?" Fenlow bellowed in a tone of triumph. "I'm disappointed that you've forgotten so quickly how powerful my computer, Succubus can be. I could order it to crush you all quite easily. But I've decided to allow you to live so that you can witness the historic victory that you ungrateful lab rats were stupid enough to pass up."

Succubus announced, "There is a second fleet of ships emerging from hyperspace at coordinates three, four, seven, three, two. Seventy destroyer class vessels."

"Vendetta's fleet sent by Carnaby," Fenlow declared. "Just as I expected."

"Vendetta? Carnaby?" Blair inquired.

"Both one in the same," Fenlow added. "Are you so naive as to think that Vendetta had completely melted into oblivion? If it weren't for Carnaby, Carp technologies and a few others bankrolling them and pulling their strings the entire organization wouldn't be able to organize a bake sale, let alone start a civil war."

"There is an incoming message from Walter Carnaby," Succubus announced.

"As I expected," said Fenlow. "Send him through."

The smiling image of Walter Carnaby appeared above Succubus' eye.

Fenlow cheerfully greeted Carnaby. "Hello Walter. You're right on time."

"We're reshaping history. I'd be a fool to be late for such an event like this. I assume that you have our Brelac allies under control."

Fenlow nodded. "Of course. The psionic jamming signal transmitted by Succubus is working perfectly. Mariner's forces have been immobilized. All that remains is to head for our prime target. But first I'm preparing to warm up with a little target practice. Succubus, give me an outside visual."

Carnaby's face was instantly replaced by the image of the blockade of ships waiting out in space. The Protectorate's enormous triangular shaped battlecruisers and destroyers were joined by the equally huge rectangular carriers. The carriers launched a countless swarm of fighter craft that streaked towards the Viperhawk with their laser cannons blazing away.

"Fire at will," Fenlow commanded.

The Viperhawk unleashed a wave of carnage as it's main weapon incinerated ten of the large ships. Their confederates quickly maneuvered to surround the Viperhawk while firing their powerful weapons. The Viperhawk proved to be an easy target to strike but impossible to destroy. It was impervious to the combined firepower that would have quickly destroyed any other vessel.

The Viperhawk spun around and fired again. This time it consecutively destroyed seven ships. The Protectorate fleet fought diligently with every available weapon against the Viperhawk but so far their efforts were futile. The wide stream of devastating energy that The Viperhawk fired steadily diminished their numbers. Among the sounds of thundering explosions the terrified screams of the dying echoed throughout the room. Panicked voices shouted desperate orders to evade the Viperhawk. The numerous fighters that circled about the Viperhawk were not immune to the carnage. The ship's multiple gun turrets fired accurately and exploded dozens of the small ships.

The Viperhawk quickly spun around to follow a large group of destroyers that were attempting to maneuver behind it. The Viperhawk fired. The destroyers all exploded in the lethal stream of fire.

Fenlow smiled, pleased with the results of this lopsided battle. "I can almost feel sorry for the poor fools. Desperately trying to penetrate the Viperhawk's shields while waiting to be swatted out of space. It's a shame that you can't see it, Mariner."

"It's a shame that I can't see anything," Mariner responded in a cheerless tone.

"You're still under the effects of Succubus' jamming," said Fenlow. "If you're willing to behave yourself then I can afford to show a little mercy."

There was a pause before Mariner answered. "You're in control," Mariner grudgingly professed. "You won't get any trouble from me or my forces."

"A wise decision," said a gratified Fenlow. "Succubus, terminate jamming sequence."

The three Brelac moved their heads about to scan the room. Colin diverted his eyes from the image of the battle outside to observe their reaction. The effect left him confused. "What did you just do?" he questioned Fenlow.

Fenlow approached Colin. "I was exploiting the Brelac's prime weakness. Their lack of eyes. The Brelac depend on their psionic implants to grant them a form of psychic vision. Succubus is able to transmit a psionic signal that effectively jams their implants. Since Mariner has decided to be a good boy I've elected to terminate the jamming. Now he and his forces have regained their sight. And they'll keep it as long as they cooperate and stay on my good side."

Colin's confusion grew. "If you have such a powerful weapon to use against the Brelac then why not use it to help end the war?"

"Ending the war in favor of the Protectorate did not fit into Vendetta's plans. When we first made contact with the Brelac we carefully negotiated an arrangement with them. We would grant their ships access to our hidden bases to resupply and make repairs. We would also grant them access to certain bits of tactical information from time to time. In exchange certain targets connected to Carp Technologies and Vendetta would remain untouched by Brelac aggression."

"So in other words you sold the rest of us out in order to cover your own asses," Colin bitterly concluded.

"I prefer to call it, buying time," Fenlow corrected. "It wasn't our goal to live under Brelac rule either. We had to work with them and keep them pacified until we could find an effective means of withstanding their power. And they handed it right to us."

"The psionic implants," said Blair.

"The implants," replied Fenlow. "A technology possessing an awesome potential. Unfortunately the Brelac were too short sighted to realize this. Otherwise they would have developed them to the level that I achieved."

Colin digested Fenlow's explanation. A sinister tale of clandestine treachery. He could only theorize about Fenlow's future plans. "So, what are you going to do after you take over the Protectorate? Create an army of Reploids equipped with your special implants?"

"No. You Reploids are obsolete," Fenlow laughingly replied. "I intend to use my Cybernoids to enhance the military forces of my new empire. They're quicker to manufacture and far more powerful than all of you combined. But then you've already found that out. I'll also need them to police my Human/Brelac joint forces and guard against any resistance. I gave you and the others a chance to join my new empire. But you spat it back in my face. Now I predict that your survival will be short lived."

"And what about us?" Mariner inquired. "Do you intend to kill us along with them?"

"No. You're still useful to me," said Fenlow. "I'll allow you to leave and go back to Rantraven. By the looks of things outside your squadron won't be having facing too much opposition from the Protectorate forces."

Fenlow's conclusion was correct. The Viperhawk continued to destroy any ship within it's gun sights. The blackness of space was alight with the explosions from destroyers and battlecruisers that would never fight again. Frantic voices from the remaining ships relayed the order to retreat. The small group of survivors began to quickly disperse as the Viperhawk continued firing at them. Five more battlecruisers were destroyed as they fled for safety.

"Succubus, cease fire and proceed to Maseklos Prime," Fenlow commanded. He turned to Mariner. "Are you deciding to stay?"

"I'll stay. I'm curious to see how this whole thing turns out," Mariner's answer.

Fenlow smiled. "A wise choice. I would rather have spectators at my side who can better appreciate the historic events that I'm about to create. Not unlike my ungrateful creations and my associate, Doctor Blair Van Doren."

Succubus announced that Carnaby was transmitting another message. At Fenlow's order Carnaby's face replaced the image of space outside.

Jubilant laughter spat from his lips. His face beamed a broad smile. "That was magnificent. That ship is more awesome that you first described to me. You went through that entire fleet like a jackhammer on an anthill. Our scanners show that they've scattered beyond the system. But they appear to be attempting to regroup and launch another assault."

"They no longer concern me," said Fenlow. "My focus is on Maseklos Prime. In just a few moments we'll see whether Drennen and the others are stupid enough to defy me."

"We'll remain a safe distance behind you until it's time to make our move and occupy the capital. Carnaby out."

Carnaby's image was instantly replaced by the scene outside. The Viperhawk was rapidly nearing the blue planet that was the center of the United Protectorate. Maseklos Prime. A planet that was now sitting vulnerable before this powerful invader. Standing between Maseklos Prime and the Viperhawk was the planet's last line of defense. The huge octagon orbital base that permanently orbited the planet.

"Succubus. Destroy that object," Fenlow commanded.

Blair engaged in a frantic struggle to break free of the wall. "Doctor Fenlow, please. There are over three hundred people on that base."

"There are even more people down on the ground," Fenlow's stoic reply.

A stream of energy blazed out from the Viperhawk and burned through the orbital base. The entire structure exploded into countless burning fragments that quickly dissipated in the cold vacuum of space.

Colin began to join Blair's struggle but it lasted briefly. The psychic force that held him was far too powerful for his puny muscles to overcome.

"The remaining units in the defensive fleet have regrouped and are heading on an intercept course," Succubus informed Fenlow.

Fenlow gave an annoyed sigh. "Give me a visual."

Succubus displayed the image of several battlecruisers and destroyers flying on a direct course towards the Viperhawk. After the merciless thrashing that the fleet had earlier endured Colin was amazed that the survivors would either be courageous or insane enough to try and wage another futile assault against this ship. He heard an array of voices barking out orders and receiving responses shouted back. There was one voice that Colin thought that he recognized. Apparently Fenlow picked up the voice as well. He raised his hand.

"Succubus, stop. Patch me into the ship that made that last transmission."

Succubus instantly obeyed, showing the image of a ship's bridge. Dozens of crew members were seated in front of their consoles. A few high ranking officers were standing behind some consoles in a supervisory role. There was one officer that Colin's eyes quickly focused on.

Fenlow boisterously called out, "General Larkin. I thought I recognized your voice. Nice to see you. If I had known that you were attending this little party I would have taken the time to eliminate every damn ship out there."

Larkin looked up, amazed to see Fenlow's transmission. "Fenlow. I had a feeling that you would be on that ship. As soon as we get within firing range we're going to blow you out of space," Larkin vengefully shouted.

Fenlow laughed in the face of the threat. "Just where were you during the last attack? In the john while working on a crossword puzzle? You were lucky to escape with your life the first time. Maybe I should give you a little demonstration of what's in store for you if you get in my way. Succubus, bring us about."

The ship turned sharply until it faced the small fleet of semi-circular ships that followed it. The ships that were manned by Vendetta personnel.

Fenlow pointed his finger at the image of three of the vessels. "Fire," he crisply ordered.

The Viperhawk's main weapon unleashed it's firepower that obliterated the three ships in an instant.

Colin was greatly confused at this new turn of events. Fenlow firing upon his allies ships? "All this power that you're wielding must be driving you insane," Colin charged.

Fenlow ignored Colin's insult, as Succubus announced that Carnaby was sending another message.

"Fenlow, what the hell's going on?" Carnaby bellowed. His face baring an enraged guise. "Tell me that was an accident or a malfunction!"

Fenlow was remaining calm and confident in his power. "I can't tell you what you want to hear, Walter. But if you need an explanation then I can tell you that there's been a slight change in plans."

"What the hell are you talking about?"

"What I mean is that I've decided weeks ago that I should be the one to exclusively benefit from this power. After all, I've done all the real work. You just sit in the safety of your cushy office and make plans. And I'm supposed to just hand everything over to you? What's my compensation out of all this? A gold watch? An office party in my honor?"

A burst of rage exploded from Carnaby. "Dammit Fenlow. You are a member of Vendetta and an employee of Carp Technologies. You work for me! Now I order you to stand down and surrender that damn ship! I'm getting somebody else to handle this operation!"

"I don't think so, Walter," Fenlow returned. He was standing firm in his position. "Perhaps you've forgotten the compliment that you've paid me earlier about the Viperhawk's power. Maybe I should give you another little demonstration to jog your memory."

Carnaby said nothing. He simply held an infuriated grimace on his face. There was no choice but to hold his rage in check or risk the threat of invoking Fenlow's wrath.

"Just keep your nose clean and stay out of my way, Walter," Fenlow sternly warned. "Just leave Maseklos Prime to me. Succubus, bring us back to the planet."

Colin was highly intrigued by Fenlow's treacherous nature. "I'm curious. Is there anyone in this universe that you're really loyal to? So far you've taken your Brelac buddies, Blair, the Protectorate, Vendetta and your boss and managed to stab them all in the back on the same day."

Colin watched Fenlow approach him. Fenlow stood a few short feet away and looked into Colin's eyes. "Your limited Reploid programming can't comprehend the concept of how to use power. When you're holding a smoking gun and half your enemies are laying dead at your feet you don't need to show loyalty to anyone."

"I understand more than you realize," Colin bitterly protested. "I understand that you have to be loyal to something or someone. Otherwise your life will be pretty damn empty."

"As empty as your life?" Fenlow chided in an irritated tone. "You and these other Reploids are nothing more than complex computer programs rum amok. But I suppose that it's all my fault. Diane and Kelly were originally part of a larger group of Reploid infiltrators. The plan was to have them penetrate Helios military base on the planet Meridan and blend in with the Human personnel as you did. But the Brelac ship that carried them was shot down and they were the only two that survived. Then you were captured by Protectorate troopers. Then we needed a little damage control to deal with that problem."

"If we were such a problem then why didn't you just kill us?" asked Colin.

"Believe me, I wanted to quietly terminate the three of you but Doctor Trevor feared that there would be too many questions. He had a better idea. He wanted to program you to be independent. To think for yourselves. Not like your previous programming, where your lives revolved around your programmed missions. Since you were programmed to think for yourselves Trevor claimed that your primary concern would be to maintain your survival.

You would refuse to cooperate with the Protectorate and not work for them. That would ultimately result in you being eliminated by the Protectorate."

After hearing that explanation Colin was compelled to admire and feel grateful for Doctor Trevor's failed plan. "That way the Protectorate would do your work for you by terminating us. A good plan. So tell me what happened to change all that?"

"What happened? Trevor's stupid idea failed. Obviously what happened is that you three formed a sort of camaraderie. You developed sympathy for the Protectorate. In short, you three rejects have become the annoyance that I've feared. But I'll deal with you after I've concluded my business with Maseklos Prime."

Now Colin had finally gotten what he had previously sought after. The remaining details about his, Diane and Kelly's true origins. Being an agent for the Brelac Colin wondered what kind of person he would have been if he were not reprogrammed by Doctor Trevor. For the first time he experienced the concept of irony. He, Diane and Kelly were originally created to help destroy the very government that they were now risking their lives to save. And the priority on his mind now was how they possibly could save it.

The key to defeating Fenlow lay in disabling the source of his devastating power, Succubus. But that same computer was firmly holding Colin and the rest of the group as it's helpless prisoners. No one could even remove themselves from the wall, let alone make a move to assault the machine. But with the next few minutes the survival of the United Protectorate, as well as their own lives, depended on Colin and his friends finding a way to free themselves and destroy Fenlow's nefarious computer.

"You'll never pull this off, Fenlow," Colin said in defiance. "It's a big Empire. Somebody will find the means to stop you."

"And who might that be? The Protectorate is already beaten," Fenlow declared. "Perhaps the Protectorate will forge an alliance with the Brelac. I'd be halfway tempted to wait around until that actually happened. That way I can prove to both factions once and for all that I'm wielding the ultimate power. Succubus, transmit my final ultimatum down to the city of Navarrone. Broadcast it on all frequencies."

Colin put his mind to work in desperate overdrive to think of some way to stop Fenlow. He needed a workable plan within the next few seconds. The sound of a loud moan caught his ears. He looked over to the source of the noise, Diane. She was regaining consciousness.

Fenlow loudly and triumphantly called out to the inhabitants of Navarrone. "Attention! This is Doctor Howard Fenlow. I am speaking to you from a ship positioned in space directly over the capital city of Navarrone. I have effortlessly penetrated the paltry defenses that were set up to hinder me. I am here to issue my final ultimatum. President Drennen and the Central Commission will address me within ten minutes or I will destroy the entire city, leaving no survivors. I know that you're listening, Drennen. Remember that you have ten minutes. Don't waste time debating."

Colin could only guess as to what President Drennen and the Central Commission would say, assuming that they would even respond. "You won't get Drennen and the others to cow down to you so easily. They'll find a way to fight you."

Diane was now fully awake. She scanned her surroundings. "My damn head hurts. What the hell happened?" she inquired in a groggy voice.

Succubus announced that an incoming message was being transmitted from the city. Colin hoped that President Drennen would not be intimidated by Fenlow enough to quickly surrender to him.

Succubus brought forth the image of President Drennen, seated at a large oval table with all eighteen members of the Central Commission. The white dress that Drennen wore gave her an angelic aura that was unbefitting of the dour frown on her face. Standing behind Drennen were several other men and women who looked as equally grim.

Fenlow issued a hearty greeting. "President Drennen. What a pleasure to see you. And I see that you have he entire gang all assembled just for me. Even Defense Secretary Crane is among you."

"What do you want, Fenlow?" Drennen asked in a cold tone.

"Nothing else," was Fenlow's only reply.

"Nothing else? I assume that you did not travel all this way, cause so much death and destruction just so that we could chat." said Drennen.

Fenlow explained, "I want nothing else because you've already provided me with everything I need. The entire central government is assembled with you. I just wanted to know for sure if all my targets are in one location. This will make my job a lot easier."

Standing behind Drennen a thin black man with glasses and receding hair stepped forward. "What the hell do you mean, Fenlow?"

"Secretary Crane. Deciding now to break your anonymity?"

Drennen and the others seated at the table all looked up at Crane.

"Don't be so puzzled, everyone," Fenlow said with a gleeful smile. "Secretary Crane is a member of Vendetta. He's been in the closet for quite some time now. He's been riding on the coattails of the original plan to overthrow the government."

Crane nervously looked about the faces in the room, who's attention was now focused on him. "I don't know what the hell he's talking about. Look at him and what he's done. He's obviously a lunatic. He's crazy."

"You're about to die and all you can do is stand there calling names? That sounds pretty damn insane to me," Fenlow pointed out. "If I were you I'd be making every effort to get my ass out of that city before it's too late."

Crane panicked and drew a pistol from a hidden pocket inside of his suit. He stepped back and waved it around the room. "Nobody move! All of you get back!" He shouted. "Fenlow, get Carnaby! I demand to speak with Carnaby!"

At that Point Fenlow ordered Succubus to end the transmission. This angered and disappointed Colin. He was eager to see the outcome of Crane's rampage. But at the same time he hoped that someone among Drennen's security forces could safely disarm the man before he caused any harm.

"I don't have time to watch the outcome of that little drama," Fenlow told his captives. "Besides, this shows me what an idiot Crane really is. Now I won't regret killing him with the rest."

"What's the point in destroying the government without even making any demands?" Blair desperately inquired.

Fenlow approached his former assistant. "Colin put it quite accurately when he said that Drennen and her cronies would find some way to fight me. They might surrender to avoid bloodshed on a massive scale, but they would never be loyal to me. I don't need to keep looking over my shoulder for potential uprisings. It would be more logical to exterminate Drennen and the others when I have them all in one spot."

Colin was confused about a key point to Fenlow's plan. "If you kill Drennen and the others then wouldn't that make the job of managing the entire United Protectorate by yourself a bit difficult?"

Fenlow spun about to face Colin. He proudly clarified his plan. "I don't intend to relinquish President Drennen and her flunkies just yet. Allow me to demonstrate. Succubus, activate Drennen program one point zero."

Colin was amazed to see the image of President Drennem's face appear before Succubus. He looked at the faces of his friends. They were equally in fearful awe of this new development that Fenlow revealed. It came as no surprise to hear the image flawlessly speak with Drennen's voice.

"My friends. Even though President Drennen and the other members of the central government are about to be terminated their presence will still be needed to maintain order following the destruction of Navarrone. To that end This simulation of President Drennen, as well as the other members of the government was created. Shortly after Navarrone is destroyed President Drennen will deliver an address to all planets within the Protectorate. She will assure the people that she, as well as the other members of the central government escaped the catastrophe by retreating to a shielded underground bunker. Then a few days later president Drennen will deliver an address that will stun the entire Protectorate."

"That address will announce that a cease fire agreement has been reached between the Protectorate and the Brelac," Fenlow concluded. "The populace will be jubilant. There will be rollicking celebrations on all colony worlds. Hopefully the mood will be so upbeat that no one will bother to question the improvements that my President Drennen will make. Such as a full scale program to create an army of Cybernoids and a small fleet of ships similar to the Viperhawk. All powered by the same computer system that's holding you morons helpless. Of course there might be a few questions raised when we announce that the Brelac will be annexed into the Protectorate under a spirit of brotherly cooperation. But none of that will happen if we keep wasting time and give our targets a chance to escape. Succubus, target the city of Navarrone and charge main weapon to maximum power."

Colin was not going to remain trapped on this wall like some helpless insect. This maniac had to be stopped before he obliterated thousands of lives. He tried to concentrate and send a surge of current through the floor and destroy the computer. "You still have a few obstacles to go over before you crown yourself king of the universe," Colin warned Fenlow. Sparks flew out from his fingertips but it was insufficient power to cause harm to a machine that can destroy an entire city. Fortunately Colin was not the only individual present who possessed paranormal abilities. "This thing can't fight against all of us together," he urged his friends. "If we fight hard enough we can push it to it's limit."

Diane, Kelly and Blair all followed suit and strained to tear themselves away from the wall. Small streams of flame bored through Kelly's clothing, out from his hands and face. Diane clenched her teeth and grunted in a high tone as she tried to move her limbs. Even Blair, possessing no extraordinary powers mimicked Diane's agonizing struggle to force his freedom. It was a noble effort that Colin hoped would not end in futility and ultimately death.

Remaining silent up to this point Mariner spoke out against the physical drama that was taking place. "You've got them trapped here. Kill them now before they break free."

"I prefer to kill them while they try to break free," Fenlow told Mariner. "These fools still can't accept the fact that they're fighting a lost cause. In spite of their combined powers they're no match for Succubus. This is no simple hunk of hardware. It's power comes from it's mind. The mind that I created. Succubus is as powerful as it thinks it needs to be to destroy any enemy. And it's confidence it always unbreakable."

Colin instantly realized that Fenlow had just given him a fighting chance against Succubus. "As powerful as it thinks it needs to be!" he shouted loudly for his friends to hear. "That principle also applies to us! Our powers come from the same source. Our minds and these implants!"

For a moment Colin felt the pressure easing up on his arms. Perhaps the combined power of the group's increased efforts were starting to wear Succubus down. Then he felt the sides of his head being painfully compressed by an invisible force. His arms became weak. The pain prevented him from generating an electrical charge or even thinking clearly. He looked over at Diane. Perhaps for the last time in both their lives. She was physically the strongest member of the team, but could she prevail against this machine that would soon kill them all? The tone of her grunting and growling changed from defiant rage to pain and desperation. The complexion of her face turned deep red.

Colin felt the pressure on his head start to weaken. Diane blared out an enraged snarl and managed to rip her right arm away from the wall. Then her right leg took a step forward. Colin realized that Succubus was diverting power from it's other prisoners to deal with the one that it considered to be it's prime threat, Diane. She pulled her left arm away. Colin felt the pressure across his body relaxing. This was all the relief that he needed.

A flash of light exploded from Colin's body when he directed streams of electricity towards Succubus. Unfortunately for Fenlow he was in the line of fire. He received a jolt that knocked him to the floor. The powerful current surged through the computer and disrupted it's systems. A high pitched screech from succubus filled the room. It's telekinetic hold on the group was broken. Colin jumped away from the wall and gave Succubus two more electrical blasts from his outstretched hands. Kelly was also free. He sent a stream of fire from his hands that burned a large hole through succubus. The computer had suffered enouth damage to render it completely disabled.

Colin approached Succubus with care. Black smoke was rising from it's column shape. Colin touched it's surface. Heat from the computer seared his fingers. He needed no further evidence to tell him that this monstrosity was damaged beyond repair. Succubus was no longer a threat but there were still several dangerous enemies in this room to be dealt with. Diane dashed to the floor to retrieve her fallen plasma rifle. She darted over to the three Brelac standing at the other side of the room. "You die first!" she shouted at them.

Mariner quickly raised his hands as if to surrender and stepped back. "Take it easy, bitch. We got no problem with you."

There was a sudden pounding on the closed door. There was one major problem that still had to be dealt with. The Cybernoids were still functional and were about to break their way inside. One of them drove it's fist through the door with no effort. Colin was not about to remain here while his executioners casually strolled into the room.

"Kelly, do what you can to try and hold those things back," Colin ordered. He needed some time to think up an effective way to fight these machines.

The Cybernoid's hand grabbed the edge of the hole that it made. It started to peel a large strip of metal away from the door. It would not take the Cybernoid long to make an opening large enough for it and it's comrades to enter the room. Diane backed away from her three Brelac prisoners and aimed her weapon towards the door, but also keeping them within her view.

Kelly rushed over to the door. He held out his hands and began to focus his power towards the door. Then a large panel of shimmering blue energy appeared in front of him. It effectively blocked off the door. Kelly had produced a barrier of carefully focused psionic energy. He concentrated his power on this energy and amplified it a hundred times over until it became a physically solid force.

This would be Kelly's greatest experiment with his power. Everyone's lives depended on his barrier preventing the Cybernoids from advancing any further. Kelly kept his hands facing the barrier so that he could continue directing his power to maintain it's strength. Now the true test was upon him. Whether his barrier was strong enough to contain three creatures who could easily demolish tanks.

The Cybernoid raised it's palms and fired it's energy bolts at the barrier. It easily absorbed the powerful bolts. The experiment was a success. The Cybernoid fired a second burst into the barrier and it continued to hold up. After absorbing a third burst a hail of small blue fragments broke off from the barrier. The pieces all evaporated before they had a chance to touch the floor.

"Colin, we've got a problem," Kelly informed him.

"I'm working on it," Colin assured him. His anxiety mounted as he pondered a quick and effective solution. He dreaded the idea of having to face the Cybernoids again. The memory of the power that these robots wielded on Trillion was still fresh in his mind. They were seemingly impossible opponents to beat. Then Colin began to wonder if the key to victory was not actually trying to destroy these monsters at all.

"Diane, we need an exit," Colin told her. "Blair, keep an eye on our guests."

He and Diane both went to the wall at the opposite side of the room. Blair kept his plasma rifle and his gaze fixed tightly on Mariner, Lagar and Danton. Colin instructed Diane to rip a large hole into the wall. Her fist sank deep into the metallic surface and her hand quickly tore away two huge sections of the wall. Behind the wall was an empty room.

"Everything under control, Kelly?" Colin asked.

"Under control?" Kelly shrieked. "I feel like a spider spinning a web around a live grenade that's about to go off."

The Cybernoid was not letting up on it's efforts to reach it's victims. It had taken a more intimate approach to attacking Kelly's energy barrier. It began to hurl a steady stream of punches into the barrier. Kelly was trying to persevere, using his power to try and maintain the barrier, but his efforts were failing. Larger fragments broke away from the barrier with each punch landed by the Cybernoid. Finally it's fist punched through, leaving a gaping hole. More would soon follow.

"Let's get the hell out of here," Colin said, pointing towards the new exit that Diane had created.

There was a loud moan from Fenlow. He had survived the electric shock that Colin had inadvertently given him.

"What do we do with him?" Diane asked.

"Leave him," Colin's blunt reply. "Leave the Brelac too. They'll only slow us down."

Kelly abandoned his weakening shield and joined the others as they darted into the next room. Without his power to maintain the barrier's stability it quickly faded away. The Cybernoids were now free to enter the room and hunt down their prey.

Colin led the group out of the room and into the corridor. It was here that he would prepare his trap for the Cybernoids, and hopefully survive the experience. He ordered Kelly and Blair to position themselves a few feet down the corridor. He and Diane would also move further away. His final instruction to his friends was to follow his lead and shoot at his target. Now all they had to do was endure the agonizing suspense as they waited for the Cybernoids to walk through that door.

A powerful explosion shattered the door into fragments. The Cybernoids stepped out into the corridor, accompanied by Fenlow. Fenlow's face was a grimace of insatiable wrath.

"Are you idiots making a stand here?" Fenlow snarled. "I was hoping that you wouldn't make the chase too easy for me! You may have destroyed my plans to build a new empire but I can still have the pleasure of watching you all die!"

"We're not here to make a stand. We're here to see you off," Colin cried back.

Powerful bolts of lightening blazed from Colin's hands and flew down the corridor. In an instant one of the Cybernoids erected a defensive shield just as Colin expected it to. A six foot square panel of energy that was serving no purpose as Colin's firepower was directed not at Fenlow and his Cybernoids, but at the ceiling above them. Remembering Colin's instructions Kelly released a huge burst of flame from his hands. Diane and Blair immediately opened fire with their plasma rifles. The destructive firepower concentrated in one spot ripped a gaping hole into the ceiling, resulting in an explosive decompression. Fenlow and his Cybernoids were caught off guard by the sudden powerful air current that pulled them off their feet. Despite their awesome power the Cybernoids were sucked up through the large hole in the ceiling and out of the ship. Fenlow went with them. Screaming to his death in the cold eternal darkness of space.

Colin was elated with the success of his plan. But now he had to prevent he and his friends from falling into the same trap that they had created. He could feel the powerful air currents tugging at his clothes. Breathing was difficult. "Kelly! We need that hole sealed!" he cried out.

Kelly heard him and complied quickly. He raised his hands and summoned his power once more. A circle of glowing blue energy appeared to effectively seal the hole. The vacuum in the corridor stopped.

Colin and Diane rushed down the corridor to join Kelly and Blair. Blair gasped for his breath, at the same time holding a broad smile on his face. "We actually did it. We saved the United Protectorate. We won."

"We can't celebrate just yet. We still have to get off this ship," Colin advised.

A sudden tremor shook the corridor. The tremor nearly threw everyone to the floor.

"What the hell was that?" Diane demanded to know.

Colin suspected what the source of the disturbance was. "That's probably the reason why we should get off this ship. General Larkin and the defending fleet that attacked this ship earlier. They're making a second attack. Only this time the ship is dead in space and has no shields to protect it."

Blair offered a suggestion. "Fenlow mentioned that those Brelac had a ship docked with us. If we can reach it then we might have a chance."

Several more tremors rocked the ship. Then the group was surprised to see a small group of armed troopers storming their way. The troopers stopped a few feet away from the group and aimed their weapons.

"Don't move!" one of the troopers snapped. "Where's Fenlow?"

Colin answered, "He just stepped out. I don't think he took a pager with him."

"Fenlow's gone," said Blair. "But we do have three Brelac prisoners waiting in the room beyond this one."

Two troopers broke away and dashed into the room. Within seconds they returned.

"There's nobody in there," a trooper reported.

"They probably slipped out through the other door," Colin's theory. "They might be getting away right now."

"We've no time to look for them," said a trooper. "We were given only a few minutes to try and find the traitor Fenlow alive. Looks like you four will have to take his place. Now we'd better go before this ship in blasted into particles. Let's move out of here. Don't any of you try anything funny."

The troopers hastily led the group down the corridor. There was a large hole in the wall waiting for them. This explained to Colin how these men came aboard. There was a docking tube extended from another ship. The troopers had cut their way through the Viperhawk's hull to gain entry.

The group were guarded closely as they were herded through the docking tube and into the next ship. Colin suspected that they were probably in the corridor of a battlecruiser. The airlock door slid shut with a metallic bang. The docking tube retracted with a loud hiss. The troopers still kept their weapons trained on the group, but permitted them to go to a small window to observe what was taking place outside. The ship was racing away from the Viperhawk. But as they drew away from the ship Colin and the others received a clear view of the Viperhawk being bombarded with multiple energy bolts from the ships that surrounded it. The resulting series of explosions were enough to shatter the vessel into several small fragments. Fenlow's ultimate weapon was destroyed.

CHAPTER 30

▼

"I can't believe that we're putting up with this crap!" Diane spat out with a piercing screech.

Colin sat at his new desk in this large supply room and listened to Diane's enraged tirade. He was certain that her screaming voice was causing the dozens of metal shelves standing behind him and their contents to vibrate. Kelly and Blair stood quietly by and looked on while Diane ranted wildly about the injustice that was inflicted upon her and the others.

"There's gotta be something we can do besides keeping out mouths shut and looking stupid!" Diane caustic outburst.

"Try to calm down, Diane," Colin told her while trying to maintain his own composure. "We have our orders."

"We have our orders," Diane mocked with clear resentment in her voice. "We risk our asses to save the President, this city and the whole Protectorate . And do they treat us like heroes? Hell no. From the moment we left the Viperhawk we were treated like prisoners of war. Then they give us jobs that were worse than the last ones they stuck us with."

It was too early for Colin to compare his new position against his old one. After the conflict with Fenlow was concluded the group was informed by a Captain that they were being assigned to new jobs here in Navarrone. Colin was now an assistant supervisor working in a military supply warehouse. Diane was assigned to a construction and maintenance battalion. Kelly would be put to work at a reception desk in the main lobby of the Judge Advocate General's Corps. A high profile position where he could be closely and easily watched. As for Blair, he was assigned to the First Veteran's Hospital as a resident surgeon.

"Look on the bright side, Diane. At least they didn't really split us up and send each of us out to different sectors or planets," Colin explained to her.

"I still say that we deserve better," Diane groused.

Blair offered a possible explanation. "I sympathize with you. After what we went through we deserve the heroes' respect and honor. But the fact behind this is that the higher up's can't take a chance and trust you three just yet. After all, you were originally weapons to be used against the Protectorate."

"So I guess that means they'll keep us separated and under observation until they need us again," Diane's theory.

"I suppose you can say that," Blair replied. "But then, you guys are programmed to think for yourselves. The question is if they call you together again will you decide to go?"

"Would you?" Diane countered. "We're in the same military just like you. We follow orders. It's the only life we know. But I'd still like to have my life as a pilot."

After hearing that statement Kelly shook his head in frustration and laughed briefly. "You're still holding on to that fantasy? Captain Diane Christy, psycho pilot. It's a fabrication."

"It's all I've got," Diane returned. There was a note of sadness in her voice. "If I really am a Reploid with a programmed identity then I just can't sit in a corner until I figure out who or what else I can be."

Colin nodded in sympathy with Diane. Her position about her life mirrored his own. "Reploids or not, we're all going to have to go forward with this. We can only improve on who we are. And look on the bright side. We could have been made to be somebody far worse than what we are now."

"You originally were," Blair added. "Fortunately the three of you evolved into something better."

Colin could appreciate the irony. He, Diane and Kelly were reprogrammed by Doctor Trevor in hopes of removing them as a possible threat to Vendetta's plans. As a result he and his friends had become a force that thwarted their greatest plan.

"And what about Doctor Trevor? As well as Carnaby, Crane and the others?" Colin asked.

Blair explained, "Doctor Trevor has vanished. Along with Walter Carnaby. From what I've been told Carnaby's secretary stated that he's temporarily away on official company business and can't be reached. As for Secretary Crane, he refuses to answer any questions regarding Carnaby, Carp Technologies or Vendetta. From what I understand Crane's attorney is trying to use an insanity defense. He states that the stress resulting from Crane's life being threatened by Fenlow caused him to go temporarily insane. He threatened the President and the Commission with a gun without really knowing what he was doing."

The frown still remained on Diane's face. "Why do I get the feeling that if they were to chose between Crane and us we would end up in prison? Or worse?"

Blair assured her, "Don't worry. Nobody is going to walk away from this incident scott free. An investigation is being launched and our testimony will help bring Carnaby and the others involved to justice. But in a small way it would seem that they have won a victory. I've heard a lot of talk about the Protectorate establishing a new program for deep space expansion and exploration."

"Expansion and exploration?" asked Colin. "When we should concentrate on the Brelac and Vendetta."

"They're the main reason. We were lucky to win against Fenlow's Viperhawk, Succubus and his Cybernoids. But our enemies could easily send more of them against us. As well as more Reploids with powers like yourselves. We don't have the ability to fight both the Brelac, Vendetta and these powerful new weapons."

On that point Colin agreed. As did Diane and Kelly.

"Then we need help," Kelly surmised. "This expansion and exploration is more about finding allies in the war."

"In an unofficial capacity," Blair stated. "It would hurt morale if word ever got out that we were desperately looking for help. We could find new strategic points in space, more resources, maybe contact alien cultures and gain new technologies. But the main hope is to learn what happened to the other groups of explorers who migrated from Old Earth. In the past there have been several small scale missions to explore deep space and find out what happened to them. But the war has placed that project on a low list of priorities. History tells that the Protectorate grew from one of six separate groups that headed out to different locations. After all these years it's possible that we could be the only ones who flourished. But if any of the other groups survived and built up civilizations that equal or surpass our own then they would make valued allies."

A noble endeavor, Colin's opinion. One that could certainly prove to be beneficial. But such an exploration would not come without it's pitfalls. Space is a vast and dark mystery. After all these years they could finally reunite the separate civilizations of Humanity. Or they could encounter a threat that could be far more horrific than the Brelac. Colin found himself being drawn to the shrouded mystery of deep uncharted space. Especially looking behind him at the rows and rows of shelves holding their goods.

Diane scoffed. Her frown remained. "I hope they have fun with this deep space exploration. A hell of a lot more that I'll have."

Colin could only imagine the level of dejection and envy that Diane was experiencing. She wanted to be a part of that exploration instead of performing menial tasks. Colin admired Diane's faith in herself. Her life as an ace pilot was a fabrication, but she was determined to live it and show everyone that she was truly the greatest. For that reason Colin hoped that his friend would one day be given her chance and not spend her life living in bitter disappointment.

Blair backed away, heading for the door. "Well, I've spent enough time here. I've got to get to the hospital and make my rounds."

"And I have to go start my new career," Diane said. Colin did not like the sadness in her voice. "If I work hard enough then maybe they'll at least give me a driver's licence."

Kelly placed a gentle hand on Diane's shoulder. "Or maybe one day you'll fly again. I wouldn't want to see psycho pilot grounded forever."

For a moment Diane stared back at Kelly. Then she formed a smile. "Thanks kid. I mean, thanks Kelly."

Kelly displayed a level of compassion for Diane that Colin did not expect. He found it to be refreshing. "Nice to see that you two can get along," he complimented them both. "I hope that this won't be the last time that I see this."

Now Kelly's face beamed a smile. "Of course not. After all, we are a team." Kelly turned and headed for the door. "Unlike the rest of you people I've got the day off. I'm going to spend the day having fun and building up some memories of my own."

Diane followed behind Kelly. "We'll keep in touch," she told Colin. She headed towards the door, stopped and hesitated, then turned back to Colin. "You know, you did a pretty good job of managing this bunch of screw ups, Sarge."

"Thanks," Colin's apprehensive reply. At first he did not know how to take Diane's assessment of his leadership. Then as he watched her leave the room he decided that he could appreciate even a brash complement from Diane. Her style may have been unceremonious but he enjoyed the intended result. This day Colin McKenzie felt good about himself.

With his friends now gone Colin stood and looked at the shelves and all their goods behind him. He picked up a small stack of papers from his desk. A list of all the items that would have to be packed up and shipped out to various destinations. The first day in Colin's new life was destined to be a very long one.